To my parents, my countless friends I've made in the industry, Nicky and Sampson-the two best dogs ever and to the best muse since Martha Gellhorn, thank you.

<u>1</u>

April 19-22

"It's gonna be a great fucking day," the well-kept and soon-to-be well-dressed stockbroker said to the mirror, like he did almost every day while preparing to hit the floor. The bedroom in his little hole-in-the-wall apartment on Manhattan's Lower West Side was adorned with several lavish items, namely the two Armani suits that cost a month's rent each but each served as a reminder that he had-at least partially-made *it*. In Michael O'Reilly's eyes *it* was Manhattan and the wheeling and dealing of working in the capital of world finances-Wall Street. Sure, his apartment was barely big enough accommodate more than one house guest and he still either rode the bus or walked to work, but Michael was where he always wanted to be, doing what he always wanted to. He wasn't in the one percent yet, but he was knocking on the door. The rush he got from closing deals was second only to the one he got when he picked up his mail every night and saw that 10014 zip. 90210 may be America's most renowned zip code, but to Michael, any zip between the East and Hudson Rivers sure as hell trumped some gaudy neighborhood on a hill in California.

In the fifteen minutes between showering and heading out the door, Michael had enough time to down the first of his nearly half-dozen daily cups of coffee while taking in the best of *The Wall Street Journal*. It was a modern tradition like no other: caffeine to get the body going and the latest financial news to ensure there wouldn't be a shitstorm blindsiding him. The internet and instant information were all around him, but the old soul loved to get ink on his fingers in the morning, and the paper copy of the *Journal* gave him that.

On this Tuesday in April, the weather was the short-lived taste of spring that New York experiences between its god-awful winters and its brutally hot and oppressive summers. Michael decided on the walkabout route to work, thinking there was no point in waiting for a city bus with weather this nice. Twenty minutes later, he was in the office, and barely a half-hour after closing the *Journal* and picking up his brief case, he was on his first call of the day. Some of the more seasoned brokers viewed their job as monotonous, but to Michael, *this* is what he lived for, and it was a fun and exciting existence.

While growing up barely an hour away in Westfield, New Jersey, all Michael-or Mikey, as he was known back then-wanted to be was a stockbroker in The City That Never Sleeps. This was especially the case after his *other* dream of playing for the New York Rangers was dashed, when, as a high school sophomore, he was cut from the elite Delbarton School junior varsity team. After his hockey career was, abruptly ended, Mikey went all in on being a broker in Manhattan, and his goals were, as one notable New York mogul would say, "Yuge." "Millionaire at twenty-six, the big 'B' at thirty-five," he'd tell anyone who would listen in high school and when he matriculated at Columbia and eventually the Wharton School at Penn. Attending such prestigious institutions was a big deal to Michael; both his late parents were, in his eyes, lowly Rutgers graduates, and while they both had good jobs that allowed the family to be upper middle class, they weren't the Trumps or the Rockefellers. In Michael's eyes, both of his parents had wasted their time, efforts, and intelligence working their lowly jobs. His father had been an accountant for a local business, and his mother, a suburban real estate agent. There was money to be made in the city and if you weren't chasing it, you didn't matter. This, coupled with the pressures of being an only child, meant it was Ivy League or bust for the young brainiac, and from there, the only place to be was just on the other side of the Hudson.

Now thirty, Michael hadn't *yet* reached his goal of having seven figures in the bank, and was obviously still more than a few zeroes away from the big 'B,' but as he had learned, life changes course, and you need to roll with the punches. Especially in the decade since he graduated from Delbarton, there were more than a few punches thrown. He lost both his parents within a few months of each other after getting his MBA in 2010, which tore the heart out of the then twenty-four-year-old. Michael took nearly a year off to cope with the sudden and tragic deaths of his two biggest fans. When he did get the wheels in motion in 2011, Wall Street was still somewhat reeling from the 2008 crash, so junior brokers had to work more hours for shitty pay with even fewer guarantees than those that came before. The first years were though; he had to live in, as he called it, 'The People's Republic of Brooklyn' for a while and even spent a year living in the Garden State's emerald city-Hoboken. But by 2015, he had his borderline studio apartment in Manhattan, and his doggedness and intelligence had him climbing the ladder at an expedited rate, especially given his rocky start.

Two hours after the closing bell rang, and nearly ten hours after he got to work, the youthful-looking stockbroker was homeward bound. He rode down the office elevator with Charles Ortoli, a grizzled veteran of Wall Street, who had seen pretty much everything in his three decades in the game. "A bunch of us are going to Murphy's for the Rangers game tonight, you should come by. You've been working your ass off and could use a drink," Charlie said, grinning. He always cherished nights that involved anything other than going right home to the wife and kids in Greenwich.

"I have a game-night date with my couch, and a bottle of Malbec calling my name."

"Suit yourself," Charlie said, exiting the elevator. "Don't be afraid to let that carefully-conditioned hair down once in a great while, though. Might do you some good, kid."

"We'll see. Go Blueshirts," Michael laughed, as he stepped into the Manhattan night and headed north towards his own little slice of the Big Apple. With the sun staying out later, the walk home might as well have been an advertisement for the New York City tourism bureau.

In New York City, one of the most notable signs that you've proverbially made it is living in an apartment with a doorman. The doorman in Michael's case was Sean Jackson, a hardened Bronx native, who took the gig as a door guy after serving twenty-five years in the NYPD. Sean was the kind of no-nonsense, yet warm and welcoming presence that personified New York City. He was as quick to make a joke at your expense as he was to tell you to pick your head up after a rough day at the office. "Have you finally made that first billion yet?" Sean asked Michael-one of his favorite tenants to rib-as he walked in.

"Vegas has even odds on what happens first-me becoming a billionaire or you and the wife actually moving to Florida."

"Hey! The missus has two more years teaching school before she can cash in her pension, and we can have fun in the sun full time. We're looking at places near Tampa and another spot near Miami, nice landing spots for ex-New Yorkers. In the meantime, I'll be here making sure bad guys don't kidnap your almighty whitey ass!" Sean said in his all too thick Bronx accent, laughing.

"Have a drink for me when you get there," Michael said as he went towards the mailroom that happened to be on the way to the elevators.

"Son, for you I'll have two. Goodnight now," Sean ended the conversation as he turned on his old AM/FM radio to listen to tonight's Yankee and Ranger games.

The mailroom was well kept, but still had a weird, impersonal feel to it. One of, if not the only thing he missed about Jersey was the mailman delivering right to the door. Having to visit a little box daily to fetch his bills, junk mail, and the occasional package was more of a chore than anything else. Today was really no different with the exception of an overnight envelope from a lawyer in Massachusetts. His Uncle Dan was a Massachusetts resident and had passed away earlier that month with no spouse nor any known children. He figured the envelope had something to with his will. Michael skipped the wake and funeral, mostly because of his work priorities, but also because he detested Dan with every ounce of himself. His uncle was, to put it bluntly, a miserable old fuck that ran a bar on Cape Cod and was as easy to get along with as a cornered possum. Michael grasped the letter but hesitated to open it until he got upstairs; whatever was inside could wait to be read until the Rangers were on, and the Argentinian wine was flowing.

Upon entering his apartment after yet another stressful, but, in his eyes, exciting day on Wall Street, the mail-including the piece from Massachusetts-was tossed on the countertop, and his $300 designer shoes were kicked across the room in a manner that would've made David Beckham proud. Upon pouring a tall glass of wine and making sure the pre-game show was on Michael carefully opened the letter and the contents absolutely shocked him. According to the Law Offices of Taylor and Harper in Barnstable, Massachusetts, the run-down dive bar that his late uncle owned now belonged to him, because he was Dan's closest living relative, and apparently, the old bastard never got around to filling out a will. Not only did Dan own the bar, but he owned the waterfront property in Wellfleet that the bar sat on; he got it for cheap in the early 1970s, and now that all belonged to Michael.

"Well, I'll be damned," he said, reading it with pure shock. All the years of silence between the two, all the years without so much as a Christmas card sent either way, and now everything Dan owned belonged to his "estranged" nephew.

By the time Michael processed everything, the Rangers were on their way to overtime, but Henrik Lundqvist's amazing night took a backseat to the unexpected inheritance that had just landed right in his lap. He knew there'd be some red tape and hurdles to climb in the form of paperwork, but with real estate on Cape Cod being a seller's market and seemingly *everyone* in New England being a raging alcoholic, there was the potential for a seven-figure payday to come from this. Possibly enough-when it was all said and done-to move uptown to the Upper East Side, which was the next step in conquering the island of Manhattan.

Per usual, Michael was up with the sun, but on this day, he phoned the lawyers in Massachusetts before he did anything else to get the wheels rolling. Luckily for Michael, Alan Taylor was an equally driven worker and was in the office when the phone rang at 6:15 am Right off the bat, Michael made it known that he wanted to flip the property, bar, and whatever else he could, preferably as soon as possible.

"Slow down for a second," Alan said. "You know as well as I do these things take time, and it'll be a few months, minimum, before we can make all these big things happen. Patience, young Grasshopper."

"You're right. I got a little ahead of myself," Michael said. This wasn't going to be an overnight thing.

"Besides, the busy season is coming up, and the place is a hot spot for tourists, you'll be printing money between Memorial Day and Labor Day. You might as well come up here in the next few days, take a look at the spot, and sign some more paperwork. Can you get here this weekend?"

"Yes, I can. I'll try to be out and en route immediately after the closing bell Friday afternoon,"

Michael said, throwing his big Saturday night plans of going to the Yankees/Orioles game out the window.

"My email is in the paperwork I sent you; let me know when you've got everything set. Looking forward to getting this done." Alan hung up. The sun had barely risen over the sand dunes of Cape Cod, and he had completed his first billable session of the day.

"How the fuck am I going to get to some outpost in Massachusetts on Friday night?" Michael said as he pondered the journey and prepared for another truly unique day on the floor.

He felt that going to work after getting this kind of news was the equivalent of opening a present before school on your birthday. Michael knew he had to go to work and do his job, but all he could think about was that present. That being said, in both circumstances, it's perfectly fine to gloat, and make yourself the center of attention on *your* day. And, oh boy, did Michael ever feel like gloating.

Once at work, Michael let his co-workers (and essentially anyone else that would lend an ear) know that he'd inherited a bar and some property on Cape Cod. Suddenly, *everyone* wanted to be his friend, from higher ups who were "tired" of the Hamptons and wanted to check out what they thought was a seaside sanctuary south of Boston, to the entry-level guys and girls who raved about spending a few summer nights on "The Cape" while wrapping up their MBAs at the Harvard B School. While almost everyone in his "audience" raved about Cape Cod and the New England coast, he still wasn't sure what to think. He had been there once in his entire life, and it wasn't exactly a positive trip, but the second-hand excitement of everyone around him made him wonder if this place was better than he remembered, and worth taking the trip to, if only to flip it for a nice payday.

In the time he wasn't on the phone or bragging about the inheritance that had fallen into his lap like manna from Heaven, Michael was still racking his brain as to how he was going to get to Wellfleet. He didn't own a car, and it's not like MTA went to Cape Cod, so it would take some real doing. He decided that flying into Barnstable (luckily, there was a 6:15 flight from LaGuardia Friday night) and having a black livery car-driven by an experienced driver that knew how to get around Cape Cod pick him up and take him to Wellfleet was the best plan of action. He wondered if going 200 miles as the crow flies in such an elaborate fashion was a little over the top and pretentious? Sure it was, but as he learned on Wall Street and in Manhattan, if you're not living big, you're really not living at all. He emailed the lawyers that he'd be at the Cape Cod Bay Inn all weekend, and they could meet there to start getting the work done. The place sounded picturesque, but the only thing that mattered was that it had a boardroom, which most places on the Cape didn't.

Work on Friday seemed to drag on forever, like the last day of a school year. Yes, this was just a business trip to a somewhat unsavory location, but the eventual payout was going to be well worth a few days in a New England fishing village. Besides, whether or not he realized it, he could use a few days out of the hustle and bustle of the Burroughs.

The 7 pm flight out of LaGuardia had him on the ground in Barnstable by 8. When he walked off the plane, the scent of salty air hit his nose, and he realized he was in a whole different world. New York's air quality wasn't as atrocious as Los Angeles', but this burst of salty air was the exact antithesis of that.

His black car was waiting for him right outside the terminal, which in and of itself was a bit of a culture shock. Unlike the big city airports he was used to, Michael didn't need to tell his driver which airline's terminal to pick him up at, as there was only one terminal in the small airport that seemed like a throwback to the early days of aviation in America, before there were as many airlines as there were species of fish in Cape Cod Bay. The ride north was quiet as Tony, his driver, seemed more interested in completing the trip in a timely manner than making small talk, which was fine with Michael.

During the 40 minutes in the car, Michael did crack the window to take in the salty ocean breezes and admire the sand dunes that lined the road under the gaze of moon and starlight. The irony of living in a place as star-studded as Manhattan is that the light from actual stars is drowned out entirely. But on this stretch of road, a proverbial Plymouth Rock's-throw from where the Pilgrims first set foot in North America, the starlight led the way.

When they pulled into the Cape Cod Bay Inn in Wellfleet, it was close to 9 PM, and, unlike most other places in America on a Friday night, it was quiet. Sure, there were a few people at the hotel bar sipping lagers and vodka sodas, but beyond that, it was dead. When he got into his room, Michael was pleasantly surprised to find not only a minibar, but a high definition television. The reviews on Yelp were hit or miss, so he was glad his room was a hit, at least at first glance. Looking at his watch, he realized he had a meeting in 12 hours, but it was still early, and The Whaler was a mere three minute walk from the inn.

"Might as well check it out," Michael said, as he ventured out of his comfort zone and into the Massachusetts night.

2

April 22

From the outside The Whaler was as Michael expected it to be-almost overly clichéd. The "W" in the sign was in the form of an anchor, and a faux harpoon hung over the doorway. Inside was a 15 person bar and about a dozen tables-none anywhere near capacity. Again, like at the inn, there were people-just not a lot of people-especially for a Friday night. There were a few families finishing up their meals at the tables, and at the bar sat about half a dozen drinkers that had a regulars vibe. The bar was tended by a short, raven-haired woman in her late 20s who, while pretty, would probably look just a little better with just little less makeup on. "Can I get you a drink?" she asked Michael as he planted himself on a barstool.

"Yes," said Michael, ready to indulge in his end-of-week tradition-ordering the classiest of drinks-despite the fact the bar was anything but classy, and the stool felt like he was sitting on a tree stump with a porcupine on it. "A dirty martini, with blue cheese-stuffed olives if you have them, please."

The bartender's face dropped as she struggled to come up with a response that would suffice the high-classed patron in front of her.

"We don't have olive brine *or* olives. The old owner didn't believe in keeping them in house and the only bleu cheese we have comes with our buffalo wings. Can I get you something else?"

"Oh, I guess I'll take a Tito's Cape Codder. When in Rome, right?!" Michael said as he unknowingly doubled down on his barroom stupidity.

"I'll get you a Tito's and cranberry," the bartender said, as she seemingly lost her patience and dropped her overly personable act. "Do yourself a favor and don't ever call it a Cape Codder ever again. Saying shit like that's the quickest way to get on a bartender's shitlist."

While she was laying the verbal smack down on Michael, the regulars starting laughing like a pack of hyenas. They had seen this before, and like any great comedy act, it never got old, and even got funnier every time it was performed.

As she turned to make the drink, all Michael could think of was how quickly he already alienated the staff at a place that he now owned. When the bartender came back with his drink, she gave him a look up and down and said, "You wouldn't happen to be Dan's nephew, would you?"

Michael was taken aback. His "cover" was blown and he was almost at a loss for words.

"Yes, how'd you guess?"

"We heard you'd be around this weekend, and that you worked on Wall Street. You've got the Manhattan uppity attitude *and* Dan's nose, so it didn't take being Elliott Stabler to figure it out. I'm Aubrey, by the way," she replied in a way that showed she had a budding career as a sleuth, in addition to her love of watching crime dramas.

"Michael," he replied reaching out his hand and a breathing a sigh of relief that the tension had left the air. "My Uncle didn't like olives?"

"Nope. He was a weirdo like that"

"I'm not that weird, by most people's standards," Michael said, trying to piggyback on the newly injected humor.

"It *is* weird to order fancy drinks in a shithole like this, but I'll let it slide this time," Aubrey said before trying to switch the topic to something slightly more inquisitive. "Did you drive up today?"

Michael damn near spit out his drink when he heard that question and with a bit of laugh reminded Aubrey of where he hung his hat.

"Own a car in New York City? God no!"

"Wait, you're obviously not poor, but you don't own a car? How the hell does that work?" Aubrey didn't know if something went over her head or if this fancily dressed out-of-towner was being 100 percent serious.

"I'll put it this way: when I'm conversing at a party in Manhattan and someone mentions living in the City *and* owning a car, I just walk away," Michael said, without a hint of sarcasm. "They're in an entirely different stratosphere, and I've got enough awareness to know I'm not worth their time,"

"I can't imagine living like that. Around here you need a car to get around. I bought my first car my junior year in high school and haven't looked back since," Aubrey said as she thought fondly of her '95 Impala.

The two talked cars-Michael hadn't owned one since grad school-and life on the Cape vs life in the Big City, for about 30 minutes, as the patrons came and went, though the bar was never more than half full. Around 10:30, a woman walked in with a strut that screamed authority, and made a beeline to behind the bar to begin counting a drawer, without saying a word. Aubrey went over to her, whispered something, and pointed over to Michael. Immediately, she went over to Michael and had a hand out to introduce herself. "Michael? I'm Christina, I'll be at the meeting tomorrow morning."

To say Michael was perplexed would be like asking whether a bear shits in the woods. Who was this woman? How did she know about a meeting he assumed was between himself and the lawyers?

"Are you sure, because I thought it was going to be at the hotel with just the lawyers and myself."

"Wow, you really are out of the loop," Christina said as her face dropped, realizing enlightening her new acquaintance would be a handful. "I was your uncle's lead waitress and interim manager here, and have been running things as he would have since he passed. He was *supposed* to have left ownership to me in his will, but like most other things with that fuck, he never got around to it."

"Oh, will you being the one buying me out?"

"Shit no. I'm coming off a messy divorce, have a mortgage, car payment and two kids in private school," replied Christina, never breaking eye contact. "Better chance of seeing Christ come down off the cross and your uncle coming back from where he went at the same time. I do have a buyer in mind, however."

Christina pulled up a stool, and without getting into too much detail, began catching Michael up on all he needed to know ahead of the big meeting. The broker from the Big Apple had been in some high pressure sit-downs before, but Christina doubted he had ever been as ill-prepared for anything as he was for tomorrow's meeting. Not only had his late uncle had peculiar ideas for his menu, but his book keeping was far from 21st Century. In the months since Danny had passed, Christina had spent countless hours transferring all his paper documents concerning The Whaler into spreadsheets. She said overall, the place was making money, but there was expensive work to be done on the septic system, which might as well have been used by the pilgrims. Every year that passed without a replacement meant the job of revamping the plumbing would only become more costly and time-consuming. Likewise, no one in their right mind would spend top dollar on real estate with such a fatal flaw.

While his ear was getting talked off about what kind of shitty business owner his Uncle was and the shitty business going on underground, all Michael could ponder was the menu in front of him. The prices were so much lower than he was used to, and the options-especially when it came to drinks-to put it bluntly, sucked. If he was going to be running this place, even for the summer, it *had* to be better than this.

"Can I come up with some new shit for the menu?" he asked. "I think it could use a little touch of civilization, especially on the drink side."

Christina was taken aback. She'd listed everything that was wrong with The Whaler, and all this out-of-towner could think of, was that the drinks sucked. But she answered him, anyway. "Sure, we can draw something up after we get all the business wheels rolling tomorrow."

It was getting late, and the few regulars had closed out and were going home.

"I'm gonna shut it down in a minute," Christina said as she remembered she still had work to do outside of chatting up her new boss. "Feel free to take a look around and get to know the place a bit."

Michael took her up on the offer and began exploring the ins and outs of The Whaler, and the more he looked the more he couldn't help but think he wasn't in the Empire State anymore. For starters, unlike the bars he was used to in Manhattan, there were no "top shelf" pours-there were only pours. No Johnnie Walker Blues, no Oban 14s, just your run of the mill boozes, and for the patronage at this place, apparently that was just fine. Around here, if it couldn't be made with Jack Daniels, Stoli Raspberry, or the like your drink wasn't getting made. Likewise, there were more obscure brands than he could shake a stick at-instead of Fireball Whiskey, there was some Irish brand that he was sure did the same thing: getting frat boys, daddy's girls, and other amateurs who can't handle *real* booze hammered-at a fraction of the cost.

Getting out from behind the bar, he saw pictures adorning the wall of everyone from Steven Tyler to Tom Brady. Big time Boston athletes and local boys who made good in movies and music were all up there. But the more Michael looked through the "wall of fame," the more he noticed one gaping omission-no hockey players were on the walls anywhere in the restaurant. Hockey is obviously the least popular of the North American sports, but having Larry Bird and David Ortiz pictures without any of Bobby Orr or Patrice Bergeron left even a visiting New Yorker feel like he was looking at old record covers of Simon without Garfunkel.

One picture that did catch his eye was that of a beautiful brunette tending bar in a beat up Power Play with CJ shirt. "Who's the cutie behind the bar in this picture?" Michael asked a still busy Christina.

"Katie Nolan, she's a national TV host from Framingham that was in town for the weekend and wanted to hop behind the bar that night. Danny, being the weird old man he was thought he had a 'chance' with her and was totally fine with it. Of course after a while he creeped her, her parents, and her brother out so much that they left and haven't come back since. It's a shame, they were really good people."

"Damn. How about this guy?" Michael said pointing to a picture of a Patriots quarterback wearing #16 in an old red jersey that team had long since abandoned as its primary colors.

"That's Zo, Scott Zolak. He used to come in here all the time when we did karaoke, down a dozen Coors Lights and then butcher 'Josie' by The Outfield. Nice guy, but not the best quarterback we've had playing around here," Christina replied as she continued shutting down the bar.

Being a Jets fan, Michael knew all too well about the damage New England quarterbacks could do on the football field, and really wanted a subject change. He had nothing against talking football, but if it got into a "My Team vs. Your Team" argument, he'd have about as much ammunition as the Salvation Army in a shootout with Delta Force. In hopes of changing the subject he asked, "Why didn't my uncle hang any pictures of hockey players?"

"He said because 'Canada Sucks and it's a foolish goddamn game'-his words, not mine. Getting a Bruins game on here used to take pulling an arm and a leg. Hell, I had to beg to get Game 7 against the Habs on here last year" said Christina, not the least bit nostalgic of the Black and Gold's heart-wrenching 2014 playoff loss. "In retrospect, we probably should've kept it off."

His uncle's second-hand statement stood out to him. He knew his uncle played a bit of hockey when he was younger. Did this hatred of hockey stem from his own playing days? Michael wasn't sure, and, at this point, playing Sigmund Freud for his dead uncle was about as useful as trying to explain quantum physics to a golden retriever. He had a big day ahead of him, and he felt lingering on the set of "Cheers" wasn't as useful as catching up on sleep. As he prepared to excuse himself from the now closed bar, Christina approached him with an old shoebox that looked like it was holding anything but the latest kicks.

"Before you leave, take this," Christina said, as she handed him the box and its sure-to-be-precious contents. "It's some of your uncle's personal paperwork. We took it from his apartment upstairs after he passed. Feel free to take a look up there while you're in town. Most of it's been cleaned out, but there's a couch, bed, a TV and an empty fridge among-I'm sure-plenty of other shit."

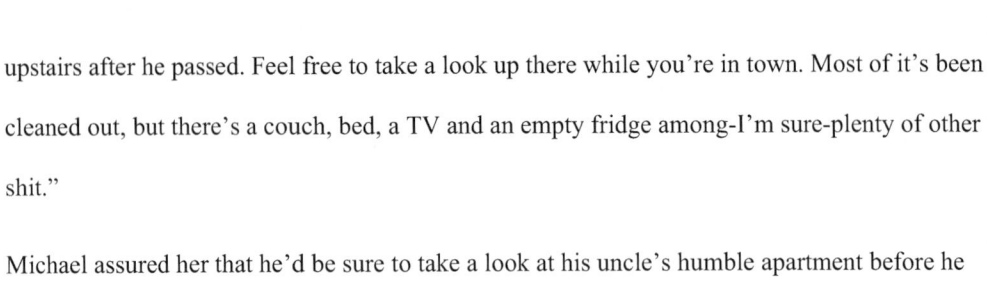

Michael assured her that he'd be sure to take a look at his uncle's humble apartment before he made his way back to the Big Apple, but that was far from the top of his list of priorities. He said his good-byes to Aubrey and Christina, and made his way out the door and towards the inn.

Walking through the seaside town allowed the salt air to really enter his lungs, and it made him sleepy like a quiet lullaby. Back in his hotel room he placed that shoebox on his dresser and hit the hay right away. The salty breezes coupled with the seemingly never-ending day had him sleeping like a baby almost instantaneously.

3

April 23

Michael's alarm was set for 7 AM, but he found himself up and wide awake more than an hour before it went off. Part of it was excitement for what lay ahead, but it more so had to do with how uncomfortable the hotel bed was. He was used to sleeping in his Egyptian linen sheets on his high-end queen-sized bed, so this twin with a mattress that may as well have been slept on the night of the Kennedy assassination was a not-so-welcome change. Despite the location and the other "amenities" of the hotel, it didn't take a rocket scientist to figure out why the reviews were so mixed.

"At least there's a coffee maker," Michael said as he put a pot on of surely only the finest variety of joe this establishment could offer, and he'd take a look at what was inside the shoebox. It would be a little more interesting than watching John Buccigross on SportsCenter talk about the Rangers' loss last night on an endless loop.

Digging through the shoebox, he found a picture of his uncle, aged 19, playing for a junior hockey team out of Quebec that more than piqued his interest. His mother had mentioned that her dickhead of a brother was a failed player of the game he apparently later came to despise. But, no matter how many of his games Michael's mother went to over the years, she didn't know icing the puck from icing a cake, so the details of his uncle's career were scarce at best. The picture was dated 1969, a time in which most kids his age were either in the Mekong Delta or getting deferments and burning draft cards, so it was, at the very least, intriguing. From what little he knew of his uncle, he knew he played and was a very good schoolboy player in Jersey, but didn't sniff the NHL, and by the time he reached 20, had given up the game. What he couldn't put his finger on was how he went from being a good young player to being a bitter old man that resented something that once gave him so much pleasure. Michael kept on digging through the seemingly innocuous items, until he found something that wasn't a run-of-the-mill crumpled up old piece of paper-the original paperwork from when he bought The Whaler in 1978 and other correspondence that pertained to that sale, which was definitely more interesting than thinking about his uncle's playing days in Quebec.

Judging from the letters and official documents, Danny bought the bar and the property in a manner that was more highway robbery than a real estate dealing as it was priced to move, and he was in the right place at the right time. Apparently, the previous owner was one of Danny's gambling buddies. He'd run up a string of bad gambling losses at Suffolk Downs in Boston, and needed to get out of the hole. Danny was fading him on his picks, and one man's loss became another's gain. Much like his nephew would learn to do on Wall Street many decades later, Danny swept in like a buzzard on a fresh kill, and bought The Whaler for what might have been grand larceny in the eyes of a more liberal judge. One thing was for damn sure-Michael took much better care of his investments than his late uncle. If he had hustled this particular bar from a fellow degenerate, there's no way it'd look as beat to shit as it did and there sure as hell would be blue cheese stuffed olives.

As the morning wore on, it was time to get ready for the big meeting. Just like any day on the NYSE, he made sure he had his "A-Outfit" on to match his "A-Game." Going back to his days as a young hockey player, he felt that the better you looked, the better you played, and he'd need that today. It may have been a hotel off the beaten path in Cape Cod, but he sure as hell was breaking out an Armani suit today. Pretentious to some, but it sent the message that he was there to kick ass and do business. He also made sure that *just* the right amount of hair gel was worn, not enough that he looked greasy, but just enough to give his naturally full head of hair a nice lift. Once he felt he looked good enough from his head down to his $500 shoes, he rode the elevator down to the ground floor and made his way toward the inn's surely-beautiful boardroom. All along the walls hung watercolors depicting various shorelines along Cape Cod. Most people would find these pictures a nice touch, but Michael-ever the cynical New Yorker-couldn't help but snicker at the mere simplicity of the artwork. Unlike the paintings that he often saw in the Big Apple, there was no story behind them, no message attached to them, just some paint on a canvas depicting seashells, birds and other "beach shit." He was no art expert, but even he could see the lack of meaning behind these generic designs.

Outside the hotel boardroom stood Christina and a pair of sharply dressed gentlemen not as sharply dressed as Michael, but compared to the rest of the locals, they might as well have been Pat Riley and Frank Sinatra.

"Hi, Michael. Alan Taylor; we spoke on the phone," the shorter of the two lawyers said, extending a hand that Michael was more than happy to shake, "This is my partner, Larry Harper. Good to finally meet you in person."

The quartet-the two suburban lawyers, the New York stockbroker and the restaurant manager entered the boardroom. It was a far cry from what Michael was used to in the Big City, but it served its purpose. A long table with 12 seats made up the center of the room and on the far end, opposite the door, was a coffee maker, a computer, a printer and two antiques a landline phone and a fax machine. The meeting opened with the lawyers and Christina explaining to Michael that outside of the outdated septic system the bar was in good shape and with a minor facelift, it could be a pretty sought-after commodity. Every question Michael had about the finances and overall outlook of the bar were answered right away by Christina, who had clearly done her homework and put the time in to understand the situation turning the lawyers into high priced spectators.

Given that the bar hadn't officially hit the market, gauging interest wasn't an exact science, but Christina said she had a buyer in mind who would be willing to wait until the end of summer to close a sale. Michael was open to this idea and told her to put the idea proverbially on ice and with a few signatures the bar now belonged entirely to him. For a guy who didn't own anything- he obviously rented in New York-owning a property and a business was now strangely empowering. It wasn't a loft overlooking the Hudson and a multi-million dollar brokerage firm, but a seaside piece of real estate and a divey New England bar would suffice for now.

Taylor and Harper seemed happy; once again they got in some painless billable hours before noon. For a duo that was used to painstaking divorce cases involving fights over the fate of summer cottages, this was the Massachusetts law equivalent of a Navy SEAL taking a shift as traffic cop.

"We're not exactly in the sales business, but through our firm we've got some leads for you to pursue," Larry said, as the quartet walked out of the boardroom.

"You'd do that for me?" Michael replied, as he was taken aback by the kind gesture that would surely have strings attached. Nothing came for free where he hailed from.

"Absolutely," Alan added, "Do you want us to set up meetings over the course of the summer, and give you until August or September to make your mind up?"

Michael thought about the complexities of taking meetings all summer, but he liked the idea. Fridays at work in the summer were a joke, so getting on a plane and being in Wellfleet by Friday night a few times wouldn't be hard to pull off. It would also take the guesswork out of having to chase potential buyers; they'd be brought right to him. "That sounds amazing," he said.

"How many meetings do you want to take?" Larry said.

Michael thought about it. Did he want a bidding war, or did he want the crème de la crème to make him an offer he couldn't refuse?

"No more than three," Michael said, as he elected to go more in the direction of the latter. He wanted to make a nice chunk of change, but didn't have time to fly back and forth all summer long. Besides, it was the like a legal version the scheme they ran in *Goodfellas* with arson and the bar after selling everything hot-at the end of the day the move was going to be a massive profit one way or the other. Going a step further, he did want to take part in the sale. Whether it was ideal or not, it was a family property and company and he took in dealing with issues like this firsthand.

"One of the regulars at the bar has shown some interest in buying it, if that interests you at all," Christina chimed in.

"Can we meet tonight?" Michael, ever the businessman, said. He would love to put the parameters of a deal in place before his visit even concluded.

"Nope. He's out of town for the weekend, but he'll be around most of the summer," said Christina. "You should take a few trips up and do the meetings. You'll get to see how the business works, too." Christina knew running a bar was a little different than Michael's typical business.

A few summer weekends spent at a beach bar, rather than in the city, would do his brain some good, Michael thought. In his still brief time on Wall Street, he'd seen plenty of talented brokers pushed to the brink (and implode) by the lack of work/life balance.

"I'd love to do that," he said.

"Good," Alan said, "We can schedule meetings around when you'll be in town and by the end of the summer, you can make up your mind and really double dip on the whole thing."

"Brendan, the regular, is going to make a real serious and generous offer, so you may not even need to take too many meetings," Christina added. She may not have had his business acumen, but she did know the lay of the land around here.

"Alrighty then, let's find two other really good offers, and I'll get a deal done before the end of the summer," Michael very politely ordered the lawyers.

"You've got yourself a deal," Larry said, knowing his firm would benefit financially from being a de facto real estate office/liaison for the up and comer from Manhattan.

Michael would retire to his room for the afternoon and do some work from the road regarding a few sales of companies soon to go public. He may have been outside of New York and it may have been a weekend, but, there was time to make at least a dent into the pile of work that would be awaiting him in Manhattan when he got back. One of the companies,-some borderline mom and pop animal feed company based out of Dallas- really intrigued him as they specialized in birdseed and given that every house in every suburb in America has a birdfeeder this had the potential to be a sneaky gold mine. Michael couldn't understand why anyone would throw bread to pigeons in Central Park, much less invite a flock to their home to shit everywhere, but there was a market there and he was going to ensure he could sell this to anyone with even a touch of interest.

During the day, he ate his meals at the hotel, because he really wasn't in love with the idea of eating in a dive bar, regardless of what the employees and regulars may have said. He realized his snobbery was coming through, but he didn't care. After reading up on birdseed and how much suburban American loves its birdfeeders all afternoon, Michael needed a drink, and there was nowhere better than The Whaler now *his* bar The food didn't appeal to him, but the notion of drinking for free, especially when drinks run $15 a piece in the city, was heaven to his brain.

When he walked in at 8:30, there were more people in The Whaler than the night before, with one exception: Aubrey. The pretty bartender wasn't in her usual spot behind the bar. She was a far cry from the Manhattan socialites Michael was used to chasing, but he realized that, despite her rough edges, he definitely wished Aubrey was here tonight.

Before he could get to a barstool, Christina stopped him.

"Do you want to bang out the new drink menu now?"

Michael's head was still deep in the birdseed world, and he'd almost completely forgotten about his conversation with Christina earlier about changing up the drink menu.

"Well, then grab yourself a drink, and meet me downstairs in the office," Christina said, as she made her way down the rudimentary stairs.

He ordered himself a vodka-cran and was at least a little flattered when the bartender, a man named David, served him his drink and called him "boss of the year," with a wink and a smile. Part of it was David's infectious sense of humor and easy-going mannerisms, but Michael, who had "owned" the place for all of about eight hours, it was a pretty cool little bit of validation.

The duo sat in the "office," which was more like a glorified server station, and went over the menu and what changes Michael wanted to see. The food, he felt, was passable as "pub grub," and traditional New England cuisine-clam chowder, lobster rolls, fish and chips-fit the restaurant's vibe to a tee. Not his tee, but a tee, nonetheless. It was the drinks that he wanted to change up; how hard would it be to order a couple of jars of olives for dirty martinis or a case or two of Corona Light, in addition to Corona? Christina took notes and told Michael that when she put the orders in, his adjustments would be made. They also talked about specialty cocktails. Michael was used to going to places in Manhattan where there was a drink you could get there that you couldn't get anywhere else. Christina was quick to point out that Danny thought such things were foolish, but now that he was in charge she'd be happy to put a cocktail menu together that catered to the audience they deal with. They brainstormed a few "Whaler Specialties" for a prototype menu, which they put into action as soon as the new items came in. Drinks like the Cape Cod Mojito-a mojito with cranberries, of course, and the Dark N' Whaley-ginger beer and Jack Daniels, would become, in Michael's eyes, anyway, a selling point for the place.

Then Michael brought up pricing "Why don't we have happy hour here?"

Christina almost fell off the old computer chair with laughter. "That ass clown, Michael Dukakis, banned it about 30 years ago. His wife had a problem with booze, and the rest of us have to suffer. Typical fuckin' liberal."

As a resident of a pretty liberal city/state that loved happy hour, Michael's most poignant thought was that Christina was a conservative in Massachusetts-which he thought was as common as a Kennedy with high moral values and a clean liver.

"Why let people make money when you can dictate minute details of their life, am I right?"

Michael said, trying his best to cater to his audience.

"Your uncle took pretty much the same stand on shit like that, and I happen to agree wholeheartedly."

"Great minds think alike," Michael replied, beginning to enjoy this back-and-forth. "Isn't that the old saying?"

"I believe so. Minds damaged by spending most of their time in this shithole start to think alike, too." Christina sarcastically retorted, and Michael cracked another smile at her not-so-subtle dig at the reality of working in this place.

"Since you've been running it since my Uncle died, I want you to keep doing what you're doing, since I'll pretty much be the owner in absentia. He trusted you, and you seem to have really done a good job, so I'm not going to shake that up," Michael said. He wanted the parameters of how the place would run to be established before he headed back to New York.

"You got it. I'll try not to buy too much stupid shit." Christina said.

"All that I can really ask for," Michael replied with a smile.

Their witty banter continued for a few minutes before Michael decided to go back to his hotel for the night. It had been another long day in Wellfleet and he just wanted to get back to New York to try to finish up the ever-tiring birdseed deal. He promised to return to the Cape for Memorial Day weekend when, the summer madness on Cape Cod would officially commence.

4

May 27

Rather than spend Memorial Day weekend in the Hamptons or on Nantucket for Figawi like most Manhattanites, Michael was back in Wellfleet to witness the annual summer party that he heard so much about. Figawi is one of Cape Cod and the Island's most storied traditions as what was once a big sailing weekend has turned into 72 hours of debauchery for every white asshole rich enough to afford a flight and lodging on Nantucket on the holiday weekend. According to Aubrey and Christina, *everyone* went—Cape Cod locals, summer residents celebrating their first weekend back at the cottage, people that hate Figawi, and people that can't afford Figawi. Given how dead the place was during his visit, Michael wasn't sure what to believe, but he made the trip just like he had the first time—a late afternoon flight on Friday, and a black car that drove him up the arm of the Cape to Wellfleet. This trip would be more pleasure than business. There'd be no boardroom meeting, and rather than stay in the hotel, he'd try out his late uncle's apartment above the bar.

Was it a bit morbid to be sleeping in a dead guy's apartment? Sure, but estrangement aside, Danny was family. It couldn't have been any worse than the inn he stayed at last time.

When he touched down in Barnstable, the first thing he noticed was how packed the airport was. Memorial Day weekend was a far cry busier than the middle of April. That fact was only further amplified when the car hit the road; the ride that took less than an hour in April took damn near 90 minutes this time around.

Today's driver, unlike the nearly mute one who picked him up on his first visit, failed to properly introduce himself, and cussed out seemingly everyone on the road. It wasn't like the rage he had seen from cabbies in New York, but it wasn't too far off, as this guy seemed as willing to drop anyone he suspected of causing traffic with the ease in which he dropped his Rs. "Fuckin' tourist cocksuckahs" came out his mouth with the volume and power of an assault rifle going on full blast. Michael lacked the courage to remind the man that he was *technically* a tourist, although, at the same time, he was now a factor to the local economy, so he wasn't your conventional summertime Cape Codder. Either way, it wouldn't have made a difference, as this man had one job-to get Michael to Wellfleet-and if it meant he'd have to drive like Dale Senior and cuss like a Lil Wayne single, then so be it, as long as he got the job done. It was no different than Michael pretending he gave a shit about birdseed to make himself money in his line of work.

The road-raged trip from hell came to a merciful end at the front door of The Whaler, but it was like he was in a different world. Not only were the roads jam packed with travelers, but there was a *line* outside the bar. Yes, the same place that couldn't draw flies in April was turning people away in May. He'd heard how busy it got during the summer, but even he was shocked, and he hadn't even stepped inside. Rather than go right into the madness, Michael gathered his belongings and entered via the side door and went up to his quarters. Christina had been nice enough to leave toiletries and other essentials in the room, which was perfect, since Michael realized his overnight bag was on his kitchen table in Manhattan, which wouldn't do him any good.

After splashing his face with cold water and getting changed into something more comfortable-a polo and plaid shorts-Michael headed down into the Friday night ruckus that was now *his* bar. As he slid through the sea of people that were around the door and reminded the gentleman working the door who he was, Michael was absolutely taken aback by what he saw-the bar was well over its "official capacity" of 150 people. After meandering his way through the crowd to the bar, he caught Aubrey's attention. He was expecting to get a warm embrace from the beauty queen masquerading as a bartender, when the clearly overwhelmed bartender dropped a bombshell on him.

"Thank God you're here!" Aubrey yelled over the loud bar. "Get back here and help me out! The other bartender got food poisoning, and Christina's on the floor by herself, and back here, it's just me and a barback who's also bussing tables and running food."

Michael was taken aback. Sure, he'd drank plenty of booze and poured himself enough, but bartending was like going from fishing for guppies in Central Park to chasing marlins in the Gulf Stream.

"You want me to do what?!"

"Come back here sling drinks, clean glasses, restock the coolers. Literally anything to help me out. I'm totally fucked right now."

What was supposed to be a casual, laid-back weekend was turning into a working one, as after a full day at the New York Stock Exchange, Michael faced the reality of having to sling Budweisers for the great unwashed of Massachusetts. Was he in love with the idea of not only working, but having to do manual labor in a field he had zero expertise in? No, but this was his ship, and he'd be a lousy captain to let it sink right now.

"Alright, let's do this shit," Michael said. He went behind the bar, and, for the first time, saw the view from the *other* side of that countertop with stools. The people were three and four deep and everyone wanted a drink at the same time. That first view can be absolutely rattling, but you realize quickly that there's nowhere to go. You can't run home and cry to your mom, you can't put on an invisibility cloak, you can't teleport to a magical island full of beers and women with loose morals; you just have to step up to the plate pour and ring in one drink at a time and let the clock wind down to zero.

A tall man in a beat up Tedy Bruschi jersey was Michael's first customer- he ordered a vodka soda. "Easy enough" Michael thought to himself. When he was finished making the drink, it was mostly booze with a splash of soda water, and no fruit for garnish-not exactly how it's supposed to be. That was only the tip of the iceberg-when it came time to ring it in, the cash register might as well have been a cryptic machine from another century. Aubrey saw this, and gave him a crash course on how to ring in and start tabs.

Even though she was completely in the weeds, Aubrey knew not training Michael on the fly on how to use the drawer would have been much worse than taking 90 seconds to show him how the machine worked.

"Alright let's knock this out so I'm not completely fucked," she said as she approached the register. Within a minute and a half, Michael knew how to ring in drinks and food, start tabs, and close out tabs. While it was not the best lesson that could be given on the somewhat antiquated computer system The Whaler had it would more than suffice.

When the impromptu lesson came to a close, Michael had one last question.

"How do I pour a decent drink?"

This was when Aubrey's patience was about to run out, as the people in the bar were only getting thirstier and thirstier. "Two ounce pours, don't forget the fruit. If it's something you don't know how to make just tell them to wait until I come around"

There weren't any jiggers to measure the pours behind this bar, but given that he aced chemistry back at Delbarton he could visually see what about 2 ounces looked like. Besides, even if it wasn't perfect, it still would have been better than the vodka with a little soda water he just served the gentleman in the #54 shirt. Sure enough, the next guy who needed a drink ordered a margarita, and once again, he was out of his element. He looked at the man, pointed to Aubrey and said, "Ask her. Or Jimmy Buffett for that matter."

As the night went on, Michael got more and more comfortable giving the people what they wanted, but he couldn't help but be in awe of how Aubrey, at 5-foot-nothing and barely 100 pounds, could be as strong and energetic at 11 pm as she was when she walked into the place. No one went thirsty for long, as she had an innate ability to cater to seemingly everyone at once. Michael was more than happy to be a support player like Steve Kerr to her Michael Jordan. He also realized the importance cleaning glassware-without it, there's nothing to pour drinks into. All throughout the madness, he was, in a weird way, disappointed that so few people wanted any specialty drinks. Sure, they'd be a pain in the ass to make with the volume, but there was a pride he felt in the bar's new drink menu, and popping Bud Lights and making vodka sodas just didn't give him the same satisfaction. He didn't have too much time to ponder why *his* drinks weren't selling, since for every drink he poured, there were two more guests that needed a refill. With the barback cleaning tables and restocking the fridges, Michael became the jack-of-all-trades behind the bar. While he was far from an industry hall of famer, he felt his presence did make a difference. Right in the middle of peak volume, the lights came on, and Michael was surprised by the sudden influx of light into the dark space.

"Why are the lights on? Is there an emergency?" Michael asked as Aubrey took a deep sigh of relief.

"The night's over. Closing time has arrived, thank fucking Christ" Aubrey said, in a tone that said 'It's 1 AM. Why the fuck else would the lights be turned on with a full house?'

Michael was now sharing in Aubrey's confusion as this was way earlier than he was used to seeing bars close in Manhattan.

"One? Are you serious? New York City's four or, sometimes even five. It's a blessing and a curse."

"Well, in this place it's one, and I wouldn't have it any other way."

As the crowd began to empty out, the crew began "repairs" of the bar-the unglamorous side of the restaurant industry that most consumers don't see. After the bar empties, the trash on the floor is cleaned up, the bottles are sprayed and wiped, and a slew of other tasks need to be completed. You don't think about the work the employees do behind the scenes to make the establishment run like a well-oiled machine when you're just sitting having a drink.

Usually, a white collar guy like Michael would be vehemently opposed to doing such menial tasks, but given that he wanted to lead by example like Mark Messier, and the fact that this bar was the closest thing to a real team he'd been on since high school, he was more than happy to whip out the glass cleaner. Sure, he worked in collaboration with fellow brokers in New York, but that dog eat dog world had very little true, blue, "everyone on the same page" teamwork, especially to this extent. Working behind the bar tonight made him long for his youth hockey days when everyone worked together to get the win-the scorers scored, the muckers mucked, and all that mattered was leaving the rink with the W.

After they wrapped up the cleaning, it was time to crack a beer and let Aubrey count out the night's tips. While Michael was pulling up a stool, the barback went over and introduced himself to his new boss.

"Hi, I'm Colin Johnson," said the youthful kid with long, flowing hair. "Nice to meet you, boss."

"Michael O'Reilly. Nice to meet you, pal. What are you, like, 12?" he said, ribbing the youngster who showed an outgoingness and sense of humor that Michael respected immediately.

"Twenty-two. I graduated from Northeastern earlier this month, and I'm working here and covering the Cape Cod Baseball League for my website," Colin said, as he proudly handed his new boss a business card.

"Baseball scout and analyst?" Michael asked, examining the cheaply put together card that he was sure the kid whipped out in bars to impress girls. "Did you play at all?"

"I rode the bench in high school at Boston Latin and my senior year got thrown off the team for throwing a party at my family's summer house in Harwich."

"Atta boy!" Michael said. He could see something in the kid that he clearly liked.

"Heroes get remembered, but legends never die and they'll be talking about that party longer than they'll be talking about what my more talented friends did on the field, the youngster replied, beaming with pride.

"It's always good to go down in history, and following the rules almost never gets you there,." Michael replied, as he raised a half-hearted toast to the kid.

The boys sat and talked sports while Christina and Aubrey did the tips and cashout. Colin told Michael he'd passed up the opportunity to sell real estate in Fort Lauderdale to barback and write about baseball on Cape Cod. When he was Colin's age, Michael couldn't wait to get paid and make a name for himself. Colin wasn't all about the money, but Michael respected the way the kid was willing to put the time in to make his goals happen, even if it was a completely different path than his.

While the duo was in the midst of an in-depth talk about the Yankees' farm system versus the Red Sox, Aubrey put a pile of cash in front of both them. Colin was elated, since he'd made more than a pretty penny that evening, and Michael was somewhat taken aback.

"What's this for?" he asked Aubrey and Christina.

"Uhhh, your work tonight? You earned a cut," Aubrey said. She was confused-why would a bigtime stockbroker be averse to getting paid? "Barback gets 20 percent of the tips, and I divvied the rest up hourly, since I got here before you."

"Yea, but I'm the owner. Isn't that a bit of a conflict of interest for me to be getting tips, too?" Michael asked, as he examined the pile of cash in front of him. For someone who worked with money for a living it was rare to see that much cash in one place.

"Who gives a shit? You worked your ass off and bailed us out. Take the money," Aubrey said, as she gathered her belongings and made her way to the door to head home. "By the way, I'm opening tomorrow morning at 10. You should come by and I'll show you a thing or two about how to bartend like a champ."

Michael was slightly hesitant to be back in the bar with so little turnaround time, but gave her a nod to say "We'll see, but don't hold your breath."

"I'd take her up on it if I were you," Christina subtly whispered as she walked by him towards the door. Michael took the hint and made his way upstairs.

The apartment upstairs was pretty much barren sans the bed, a couch and the TV, but the simplicity was something Michael enjoyed. For a guy who'd decorated his apartment to the nines, seeing empty walls was a bit of a change, like so much else on this trip.

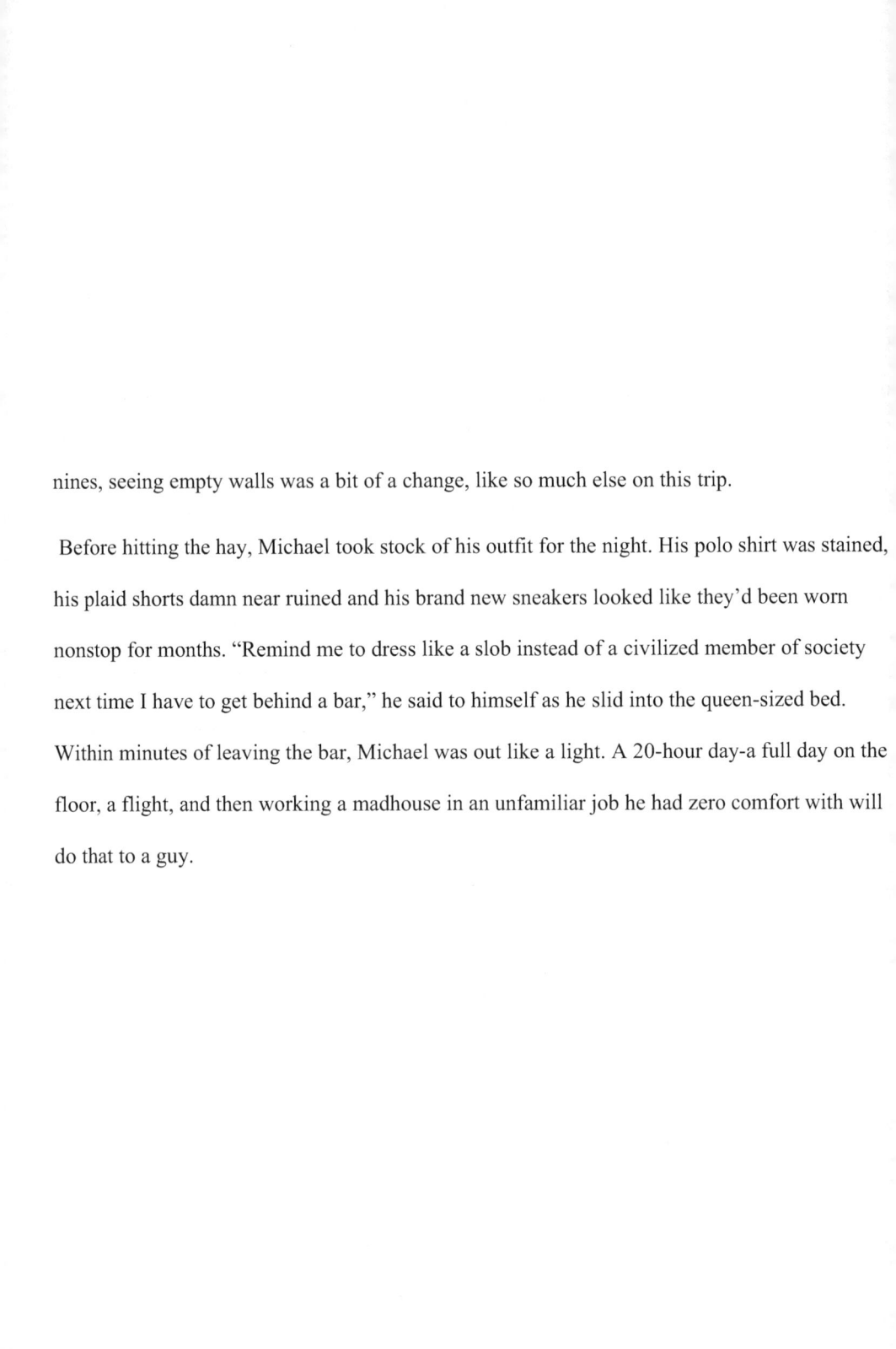

Before hitting the hay, Michael took stock of his outfit for the night. His polo shirt was stained, his plaid shorts damn near ruined and his brand new sneakers looked like they'd been worn nonstop for months. "Remind me to dress like a slob instead of a civilized member of society next time I have to get behind a bar," he said to himself as he slid into the queen-sized bed. Within minutes of leaving the bar, Michael was out like a light. A 20-hour day-a full day on the floor, a flight, and then working a madhouse in an unfamiliar job he had zero comfort with will do that to a guy.

5

May 28

Michael was up at about 9:30 and after a quick shower, made his way downstairs-not only to take Aubrey up on her offer, but because his apartment lacked a coffee maker, AKA the water-of-life-maker. As he made his way downstairs, he found it doubtful that Aubrey could already be there after a seven hour shift of nonstop work and getting out at 2 am, he figured she'd be moseying in a little later.

Sure enough, just before, 10 am, there was Aubrey, cutting fruit and icing the wells for what was sure to be another busy day at The Whaler.

"I thought you'd pussy out," she said as Michael, still physically reeling from the ass kicking he took the night before, pulled up a barstool. "You looked like a fish out of water, but God bless you, you never ran away. Here's a little thanks for your struggles," she said, as she placed a tall Bloody Mary right in front of him.

"Thanks. Usually when I'm this banged up after a night at the bar, my bank account is the one that *really* got their ass kicked," Michael said, as he took a long gulp out of his cocktail.

"You do this long enough and you get used to it. Even the most painful nights," Aubrey replied, sympathetically. "Let's show you to make a margarita so we don't have a repeat of last night."

"We can't just buy the mix?" Michael said as he knew school was about to be in session and he wasn't exactly in a mood for learning.

'Nope. For all the faults Danny had, he really believed that making margarita and bloody mix by hand was the only way to go. Store bought shit just didn't cut it with him, and as much of a pain in the ass as it could be when you're busy, it really makes a world of difference, taste-wise. The lime juice comes freshly squeezed from a market in Plymouth, because I did tell him that if we ever had to squeeze our own limes during busy season, I'd quit."

The two went over different drink recipes and the little tricks a bartender picks up while working in the industry-everything from the amount of brine to use in a dirty martini, to the fact that any bartender that shakes a Manhattan should sent to prison for destroying the drink. It really was an eye-opening experience for Michael, as he gained a whole new understanding of the drinks he'd been drinking for over a decade.

The first guest of the day walked in, and, sure enough, wanted a margarita-up-at 11:30 am. Once Michael got over how aggressive the drink order was, he whipped up one up in martini glass that would make Jimmy Buffett proud. As he placed the drink in front of the guest, he marveled at it for a split second, the way he thought Picasso probably looked at his first painting. His pride only grew when he got the thumbs up from the lady who clearly enjoyed the first of what he could tell would be many cocktails on this beautiful morning that segued into an even more beautiful afternoon.

Later, Michael sat at the bar and watched how Aubrey handled the lighter volume of the day shift with the same acumen she used with a full house. Where last night she was keeping personal interactions to a minimum and just making drinks and moving on, today she was meticulously tending to every person that sat in front of her. Make no mistake; she wasn't a person to be messed with, as Michael learned when he'd first met-she had no issue telling a frat boy that was hitting on her to fuck off-but in terms of TLC and warmth to her guests, and especially her regulars, she had a much more tender side. No water went unfilled and any guest that had a question about the menu got a thorough answer and walk through, complete with suggestions from Aubrey. Watching her and the young servers who were there for the summer gave Michael a nice insight into how exactly a place like this ran. It's not going to be busy 24/7, but with enough effort and care, money could be made on even the slowest shifts. While she was opening yet another beer, Michael asked the question that was on his mind all night.

"Why don't *my* drinks sell that well?"

"They do sell, just not like they would in other places. This isn't a craft cocktail bar; I can make a craft cocktail with the best of them," she replied, while popping the tops off four Buds in a row, "but these people aren't asking for mojitos or old fashions. It's Buds and vodka crans all day for these guests."

Was it a tough pill for Michael's pride to swallow? Sure, but he got where she was coming from. In the same way he'd order a Rob Roy in New York, a local here would want a vodka tonic. Their lack of taste for the finer things showed how uppity he was, but at the end of the day, it really came down to personal taste

By 2 pm, he had a little game going with himself in terms of guessing whether a guest was a local or a tourist by what they were ordering. What he quickly established was the few specialty drinks they sold were to the out of towners, and the real locals that the business was built upon liked things simple. Like most bars, there's money to be made by those passing through, but it's the regulars-the Cliffs and Norms of the world-that keep places afloat year after year.

Michael may not have had a lot of experience in the bar business, but it was clear to him that the people who came around a lot came because of the experience and warmth they felt from the staff. At 5 pm, a pair of bartenders-David and a fresh-out-of-college young lady named Nikki-came on to relieve Aubrey. Michael took part in the "changing of the drawers" and it came as no surprise to him that despite it being an average lunch, Aubrey still made a decent amount of money because of the charm and attention to detail she showed every guest that sat in front of her.

As Aubrey was gathering her purse and her other belongings, Michael stopped her.

"Do you want to go out and grab a bite to eat tonight?"

"Like a date?"

Despite slightly different circumstances this time around, Aubrey had been asked out by yet another out of towner, which, in her eyes, was a summer tradition like no other.

"I don't shit where I eat; Especially not with a boss, no offense. I learned my lesson when I was working back in Boston a few years ago."

"None taken," Michael said, as if he was trying to find a polite way of saying he usually dated high-end women in Manhattan, not bartenders on Cape Cod. "I really wasn't thinking of it as a date either. Just a bite to eat, anywhere but here."

If that's the case, then sure," she said as she exited stage right after yet another long ass shift at her home away from home. "Meet me at the Lobster Well down the street at 7; I'll get us a nice table."

Michael was dressed like he going out for a steak at the Ritz when he walked into the somewhat divey place. It was slightly classier than The Whaler, and was packed to the high heavens.

He found Aubrey in a stunning sundress, getting herself a drink at the bar. He walked over to her and sure enough, she had gotten a round for both of them.

"I thought you said you could get us table in here," he said as the place was only getting busier, and the odds of getting a table before 10 looked about as likely as Leo Dicaprio and his latest conquest walking through the door.

"I already did," Aubrey said as she sipped her vodka tonic and pointed to a vacant two-top by the window that offered a perfect view of Cape Cod Bay and a sunset that was something out of God's personal coloring book.

"Ahh. I stand corrected," Michael said as he had plenty of egg of on his face. "How'd you pull this off?"

Aubrey could just smile as they approached the table. "Us industry folks stick together and take care of each other. I'll buy the staff here a couple drinks when they go to The Whaler, and they repay me when I'm in here. Your Uncle wasn't well liked by other owners, or, you know, really anyone, but the bonds between industry members are always strong."

"Any specific reason he didn't get along with the other local restaurant owners?" Michael asked, though he wasn't sure he wanted to hear to answer.

Aubrey thought for a second of all the little cheap shots Danny pulled on other establishments in the area and narrowed it down to her favorite three.

"Let's see; he claimed the place we're at right now was running an illegal gambling ring when they had a fantasy football draft party three years ago. And he called the cops on Bayside, another bar in town, for having an underaged server that wasn't actually underaged, but it was a bit of a pain in the ass for the owner. And, of course, my personal favorite: trapping mice in his own restaurant and leaving them in other places, and then calling health services. Little things like that."

"He was one ruthless son of a bitch." Michael thought out loud as he realized not only how fucked his Uncle's tactics were, but that in any line of work-his own included-such cheap shots go down, and are somewhat commonplace. Then again, even *he* wouldn't use dead rodents to help close a deal, even though there sure as hell were enough vermin crawling around Manhattan that he could package up.

The two sat down, and almost immediately a complimentary round of appetizers came out. Aubrey really was a bit of a VIP in here. Raw oysters and a pot of steamers in a buttery stew on the house were typical dishes around here, but these were tasty ones, and if they were any fresher, they'd still be under the Massachusetts mud.

As he began to dig into the shellfish, he figured he'd ask Aubrey the big question that he'd been saving forever.

"How does someone as smart and pretty as you, with such a wide worldview end up working in a shithole like The Whaler?"

She couldn't help but chuckle. While his wording it may have been a bit crass, he sure as hell was on to something.

"Well, when you put it like that, I grew up in Marshfield, which is a WASP-y town south of Boston. Got a business degree at Suffolk, and jumped right into bartending-the 9-5 shit just wasn't for me, and I knew that before I walked across the stage at graduation." Aubrey paused to reflect on the whirlwind the six years since her college graduation. "I was living in Boston and working at a busy place near BU for a while with two of my friends from college. They both moved to LA two years ago, and rather than go with them or stay in Boston, I came down here, started working for your uncle and the rest is history. A twisted, at times borderline insane history, but history nonetheless. Let me guess; you thought I flunked out of hair school?"

"No. I really didn't know what to think when I met you," Michael dishonestly said, knowing she wasn't too far off from the first impression he had when they met.

As she laid her story out there Michael gained a new perspective into the life of someone he was quickly coming to like. He had judged a book by its cover and was sorely mistaken. This wasn't some dumb bimbo that couldn't read or write as she head as much class and intelligence as any woman around. The topic deviated to how Michael went from playing youth hockey in North Jersey to wheeling and dealing like Leo in *The Wolf of Wall Street*. He was hesitant to get into how fucked the family relationships were that led to him inheriting a bar from a guy he had barely known and could barely remember, because, quite frankly, he wasn't totally sure himself.

The O'Reilly family situation really didn't matter to Aubrey. She had gotten to know Danny, and could understand why he wasn't Mr. Popularity, but she also had a soft spot for the old SOB.

"How do you like staying in your Uncle's old apartment?" she asked Michael as their appetizers were bussed away.

"It's not too bad; it's really spacious up there, especially with so little furniture. Kind of dreary, but not the worst place I've ever stayed."

"Upstairs used to be a lounge of sorts that was separate from the bar, and raked in some really good money. I guess a few years ago-before I got here-Danny gutted it and turned it into his own apartment so he didn't have to commute from Hyannis anymore."

"So he was fine losing money in order to shorten his commute from 50 minutes to 50 seconds?"

"Pretty much. He could've rented anywhere for cheap, but like one of your fellow favorite sons of New Jersey he had to have it his way, and ended up costing the place money, which at the end of the day was really *his* money."

The businessman in Michael couldn't begin to process how Danny went about gutting an asset that was making him a decent amount of money, just to live above his business. "Did he ever tell you why he did that?" Michael asked, wanting more insight, however limited, into Danny's thought process.

"Yea. He basically said he knew he didn't have too much time left, and wasting it in a car going to and from work wasn't how he wanted to spend it," Aubrey said, as she reflected on the weird friendship she developed with her late boss, who that many others would describe as coldhearted. "It did kind of pay off at the end for him when the cancer really limited how much moving he could do. I swear being that close to the action is what kept him alive for those last few months."

They got a lot deeper in conversation than they did when they first met, as tales about cars and life in the Big Apple gave way to how they got to where they are and what was next. Michael talked about wanting to be Rich-with a capital R-and climbing the ladder on Wall Street was his way of getting there. Aubrey countered with how much she genuinely enjoyed being a bartender, although, due to pressure from her family, she was looking to change some things up, and maybe get into real estate or some other more "glamorous" line of work for a college graduate. Her parents were the typical country club type. They felt that saying "my daughter is a bartender" reflected negatively on them and how they raised her. She didn't say she was thinking of leaving industry to Michael, as she had been playing that close to the chest, but she did say that she wasn't seeking her parents' approval. Their thoughts on what she did with the business degree she worked her ass off for were far from the top of her mind. They enjoyed a pair of New England specialties; Aubrey had the baked stuffed lobster, Michael the surf and turf with fried oysters. The food was as good as the view for Michael, as Aubrey had cleaned up for the occasion, but at no point did she give him the vibe that she was interested in him. When the bill came, Aubrey reached for it before Michael's reflexes from years of playing hockey snatched it from her.

"What're you doing?" He said with a tone that was almost reminiscent of Billy Zane's character in *Titanic*. "A Gentleman always pays."

Aubrey's eyes rolled to the back of her head as she just shook her head in disgust. "Yea, you're right on *dates*. Last time I checked this wasn't a date. Remember?"

"Yes, I do and you're right. But let me get this tab. It's the least I can do for letting you show me this amazing little place."

"Fine. But don't forget for one second that I, too, work for a living and don't need anyone, not even Manhattan bankers, buying me dinner to woo me."

"Well, I'm a broker," Michael said. Once again, his verbiage and tone made him look like a total dick.

"You just proved my point," Aubrey snapped as Michael continued to not do himself any favors as he put his "black card" on the table to settle the bill.

"I don't try to be a dick, I think it's just a culture thing," he said as the server took his card and went to run it.

Aubrey had a laugh at his witty line that she wasn't sure was intentional, but that was why she was so intrigued by him despite his uncanny ability to put his foot in his mouth in a manner that would make John Mayer look like the Pope. When the server returned to the table with his card and the bill, Aubrey chimed in to remind Michael where he was and who he was amongst. "Don't cheap out on the tip," she not-so-subtly said to him as he stared at slip in front of him.

"Yeah, 25 percent," he said, matter-of-factly, and almost proudly, as he was upping the ante from the usual 18-20 percent.

"Industry standard is 30 percent, and this meal was a little more than standard, so don't sprout gator arms all of a sudden," Aubrey said as she slipped into the role of heel/shit stirrer, just to see how Michael would respond.

He rolled his eyes at Aubrey and put pen to paper. "I'm leaving a tip of thirty three point three repeating. I'll let them be the judge of how many decimals they want to go."

"Wouldn't have had to leave such a big tip if you let me pick up the tab," Aubrey said as she had to get a little jab in there at the end.

"It's fine. I'm not mad." He said sarcastically with a devilish grin, as the two made their way for the door, bidding adieu to the employees as they ventured into the Cape Cod night.

The "odd couple" that wasn't really a couple walked through the streets of town as the warm air of earlier turned to a chilly sea-breeze-infused evening. That's the reality of the summer months on the New England coast-matter how hot it gets during the day, the temperature drops like a rock at night. The reality struck Michael quickly; he shivered from his lack of outerwear, while Aubrey looked as comfortable in her stylish Banana Republic sweater.

Finally Aubrey relented. "Do you want to borrow my sweater?" she asked with only a slight hint of sarcasm.

When faced with the reality of freezing his bag off or wearing a woman's sweater-and therefore taking the sweater away from said woman-Michael chose to be an alpha rather than a beta. "I'll survive, hold on to your sweater. Besides, probably not my size anyway."

"Good answer. If you wanted the sweater, I would've give it you and simultaneously kicked you in the balls for being such a pussy."

"I'm glad. I chose wisely."

She laughed at his humorous answer and unintentional Indiana Jones quote before her face dropped.

"Look, I had fun tonight, but I don't think doing stuff like this is a good idea for either one of us. I'll talk to you all day when I'm behind the bar, but I just don't think we should be having rendezvous like this. Even as friends."

In all of the gallivanting he had done through college and as a broker in Manhattan Michael hadn't exactly grown used to rejection. Aubrey had laid out the parameters before they went out, but this was the very definition of doubling down.

"Oh, alright...I mean, I'll be in New York most of the summer anyway," said Michael, trying not to sound disappointed, and failing. "So it's not a big deal at all."

"Now that that's straight, thanks for a fun night, boss. I'll see you at work," she said as she got into her white Jeep Cherokee. She looked at it the way others her age would look at one of their children or their significant other.

"See ya around," Michael said, as she pulled away and he turned to enter The Whaler, which was just as busy on Saturday as it was on Friday.

Navigating through the packed bar, Michael made his way downstairs to the office where he found Christina doing inventory and other assorted "behind the scenes" work.

"I take it she hit you with the sledge hammer," she said to him, without ever taking her eyes off the computer screen.

"We just went out as friends, not really anything more, so no, not really," he replied, even though he knew he was lying to both himself and Christina.

"Don't shit a shitter, kid," Christina said as she looked up from her computer and put her glasses on top of her head. "She does that to everyone who tries to get close to her. Don't take it to heart."

"I promise I won't," Michael said as he desperately tried to change the subject. "By the way, how'd you end up working with my Uncle?"

"I owned my own place in Plymouth that went under right around the same time I got divorced. I knew Danny a little from living down here years ago, and he needed someone to run this place. For as screwed up as he was, he took care of me. All I had to do was run this place within his system, and we got along really well."

"So that's why you never pressured him about the olives?" Michael asked as he tried to weave some humor into what was a pretty sincere conversation.

"Yeah." Christina began. "I'd risk my job for a lot of things, but olives and blue cheese sure as hell aren't two of them."

"Well, that's one hell of a philosophy to have," Michael said as checked the time. It was getting late, and he had an early flight back to the Big Apple. He hated clusterfucks, and travelling on the Monday of a long weekend from a touristy region to the biggest city in North America was just that-a clusterfuck. That's why he was ducking out of dodge Sunday morning.

"Do you need a ride to the airport tomorrow?" Christina asked. "I'm free all morning."

"No, thank you. I have a black car picking me up. Appreciate it, though."

"You got it, Mr. Gekko." Christina said with a wink. She wouldn't say it, especially to someone who was, for all intents and purposes, her boss, but this type of unintentional snobbery was a big reason why Aubrey wouldn't even float the idea of seeing him on any sort of regular basis. Michael was clearly a nice guy, who Christina sensed meant well, but all the years of being in the concrete had molded him into someone very different than the type of person Christina and to a certain degree Aubrey were used to.

Michael gave her a nod and retired upstairs for the evening. The Cape and its people were growing on him-though he'd never admit it-but he still longed for Manhattan and the rat race he had grown to love. Getting back a day and a half earlier meant he could get some work done ahead of a busy week and enjoy a Memorial Day matinee game in the Bronx as the Yankees were on a heater.

6

May 31

The Tuesday after Memorial Day is in the bottom 1 percent of the year when it comes to productivity in the workplace, and for Michael, this year was no different. Not only was Michael feeling his whirlwind of a weekend, but his cube neighbor, Nick, was peppering with him questions about his weekend and the bar itself.

"So are you gonna straight up sell the place, or are you holding on to it?" Nick asked as he pressed his coffee mug to his lips.

Michael had a bit of a laugh. "The best of both words. Hold on to it over the summer to make some money while it's in season, then flip it for a nice profit when the fall rolls around."

"That's a nice setup. Any buyers in mind?"

"I'm meeting with buyers all summer, then towards the end of the summer, when I've made my final decision, I'll sign it over to whoever made the best offer. Believe it or not, owning a bar in Cape Cod is something a lot of people want to do."

"So you're having a summer long season of *The Bachelor*, only instead of a rose and a lifetime of wedded bliss, you end up with a seaside bar?"

In his almost three decades on the planet, Michael hadn't watched a second of reality TV, so the reference mostly went over his head, but he did get the gist of it.

"Yup, and it'll make for slightly less shitty TV in the process."

"Don't knock it until you watch it," Nick retorted.

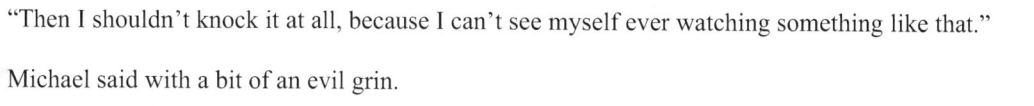

"Then I shouldn't knock it at all, because I can't see myself ever watching something like that." Michael said with a bit of an evil grin.

"You're a fresh one," Nick said with the same devilish look Michael gave him before adding, "How far is it from Provincetown?"

"I'm not sure." Michael said, since Cape Cod's geography wasn't his strongest suit, even though he now owned property there.

"Well, my husband Brad and I go up there every summer for a weekend, and if you're up there, you should come up. We have so much fun."

Michael thought about Nick's offer for a second. Him and Brad were both awesome people and they both knew how to have a good time. Besides, it meant he'd be able to be in the area and amongst fellow New Yorkers. "I'll take you up on that. When will you guys be up there?"

"A few weeks after the Fourth of July," Nick replied.

"Then I'll be up there, and we can have some fun."

"Sounds good," Nick said as he headed back to his cube.

"Five more weeks until I'm back on the beach," Michael said as he started examining spreadsheet after spreadsheet, knowing that the never ending supply of work was waiting impatiently for him. The reprieve that would come via the Fourth of July couldn't come soon enough.

7

July 3

Massachusetts is the birthplace of America and the cradle of American democracy and those Massholes know how to celebrate the Fourth of July like no one else in the country, as Michael was soon to find out. The flight from LaGuardia to Hyannis and black car to Wellfleet was becoming as familiar a route to him as his morning walk or bus ride from his Manhattan apartment to his cubicle. The celebrations on the actual holiday pale in comparison to what goes down throughout the Bay State on the night before, so to Massachusetts residents, the country may as well have gained independence on the third of July. The actual holiday is relatively tame, and would allow Michael to meet with the first potential buyer, a local restaurant guru that had some pretty deep pockets.

When he got out of his car on the evening of the third and went through the side door to the bar to put his bags upstairs, all Michael could see were the waves of people everywhere. Sure, he had seen the area crowded on Memorial Day Weekend, but this looked more like the buzzing streets of the Big Apple than a beach town in New England. As he went downstairs into the shitshow that was the bar, he was taken aback not only at the capacity crowd, but by the people waiting in line to come inside. He had obviously waited in line before, but for high end places to chase socialites and enjoy the finer things in life, not to slurp Budweisers amongst the great unwashed.

"Fuckin out of towners!" he heard a voice that sounded distinctly like Christina's yell as he prepared to enter the mosh pit/bar.

"What's going on?" he asked as he found Christina in the sea of humanity.

"Nothing, it's just these fucking kids have no respect for anything. They're down here drinking on mommy and daddy's dimes and think it's their God given right to act like fucking mongrels. Your Uncle would have already had a conniption by now," Christina said as she quickly got Michael caught up on the night's happenings.

"Wow. Is there anything I can to do help?" Michael asked, not knowing what that answer to that would be.

"No," A slightly calmer Christina replied, "but I do have someone I want you to meet."

"Who?"

"Brendan, one of the regulars. He's the guy I said was looking at buying the place and will give you, what I think is a really good, solid offer," Christina said as she continued to scan the crowd for him. "There he is," she said, trying her best to wave him over across the crowded room.

Luckily, Brendan was about 6'4'' and could see Christina's tiny figure calling him over. As he approached, Christina suggested they go into the basement office, rather than have a conversation that involved screaming and being drowned out by the music and crowd noise. As the trio made their way downstairs, Christina made the introductions and, as usual kept them short and sweet.

"Michael, meet Brendan; Brendan, meet Michael."

"Nice to meet you," Brendan said as the two shook hands at the bottom of the stairs. "I knew your Uncle for a really long time."

"I'm sorry to hear that," Michael said, as his trademark big city wit was front and center yet again.

"You should be," Brendan replied with a smile. "The guy was a prick of misery that I swear could've wiped the smile off Magic Johnson's face."

"So, Christina tells me you'd like to buy the bar," Michael said as he looked at this tall and sturdy man with beat up jeans and work boots that sure as hell were not brand name. He wanted to cut to the chase and get down to business, even on a holiday weekend.

"I would. I've got the paperwork-and how I want to make it happen-at my place. If you want to swing by this weekend, I'd love to go into some real details with you."

Outside of his already scheduled meeting Michael had wanted to take it easy all weekend, but he was interested in hearing what Brendan had to say.

"Maybe not this weekend, but before the end of the summer, for sure," Michael answered. Hopefully, he'd have the bar sold before he'd have to break bread and talk turkey with a townfolk over the sale.

"You got it pal. I'll make sure Christina gets you my information, and we can get to work," Brendan said as he headed back upstairs, Budweiser in hand.

"Hey, if you don't mind me asking, what do you do for a living?" Michael asked in a manner he wrongfully thought wouldn't make him look like a complete and total arrogant prick.

"I'm an electrician," Brendan proudly answered as he made it back upstairs and into the fray before Michael could offer a similarly judgmental follow up question.

Michael stood there with his hands on his hips at the bottom of the stairs and chuckled to himself.

"An electrician? No way in hell can give me anywhere near the number I want."

Within a matter of moments Michael had followed Brendan into the fray, and was amongst the crowd of people who had transformed from beach goers during the day to bar patrons at night. Again, being in a crowded bar was nothing new to him, but the fact people were so excited over what he thought was such a mundane place was something he didn't expect. He meandered his way to the bar where he found Aubrey-who, if she was weeded, it sure as hell wasn't showing. "What do you want, Mike?" she yelled through the crowd.

No one ever called him "Mike;" it was "Mikey" when he was a kid, and "Michael" these days. Never Mike. Even still, he wanted a drink and she was busy, so he had to make his order fast. "Vodka cran," he yelled back.

As he waited for his drink, he looked at all the people in the bar wearing tank tops or "wife beaters" as they were known in his parts-it was a beach bar, but it wasn't exactly spring break in Cabo, either. Either way, he figured their money was green, and a good portion of it would be headed right into his bank account when it was all said and done. He got deeper and deeper into his analysis of the crowd when he heard Aubrey's voice pierce through the crowd. "Ask and ye shall receive," she said, as she handed him his drink.

For the rest of the night he awkwardly sipped his drink and tried to avoid contact with anyone. There were pleasantries with the staff, of course, but for the most part he kept to himself and just observed the happenings. When the lights went on at 1 AM and the crowd began their exit-an exodus that would make Moses proud-no one was happier than Michael, as he could finally sit comfortably at the bar he owned. That was part of the beauty of being a bar owner, he found out-when the hordes left, he could stay and drink as late as he wanted to, and on a night like tonight he planned on taking full advantage of that.

In the midst of sitting and relaxing, Christina came up to him to talk shop. He really wanted nothing to do with business at 1:30 am after a full work and travel day on the night before a holiday, but he also didn't have the heart to tell her no. She was doing a fantastic job at running the bar, and by simply attaching his name to the place, coupled with a few visits over the course of the summer, his bank account was benefitting. Michael was only half listening as she repeated pretty much everything she had said in the series of emails they were exchanging regularly, and did his best to appear interested in every word. Pretending to care without really giving a shit was something that had become pretty easy to him living and working in New York.

"Oh, have you and Brendan set a date to talk about the sale?" Christina said as Michael was taken back to reality.

"Not yet, we said we'd talk about it when I'm back in town later this summer. I've got the Bennett guy coming by tomorrow night, by the way," Michael said, as took a sip from very strong vodka cran.

"I know he's coming by at 4. Good on him for taking time out of the big weekend to meet with you," Christina replied. "But make sure that meeting with Brendan gets set up. He's got a really good offer for you and he knows the people and area pretty well, so he'd do a good job."

Michael wanted to crassly remind Christina that Brendan was a laborer with blue collar money-maybe a lot of blue collar money-but he very much doubted the offer would be better than the offers the lawyers said they'd line up for him. "Will do," was all he could come up with.

While their conversation was going on, Michael kept an eye Aubrey as even after a long day of working in a filled-to-the-gills bar, she looked stunning. She was the type of beauty that could dress up and look better than the best of them, but even after long, hard hours of work, she still looked amazing. She'd been clear that pursuing anything with an out-of-town boss wasn't something she had any interest in, but he felt her look over at him a few times, too.

"If only the circumstances were a little different," he thought to himself as he prepared to hit the hay for the night. "'Night, everybody," he said as he went upstairs to retire for the evening.

He slept like a baby that night and didn't think it was necessary to leave the apartment until almost noon, which was more than a slight deviation for a morning person like him. It was America's birthday, and while he was surely proud to be an American, the day really didn't mean a whole lot to him anymore. Growing up, he always spent the holiday either on the Jersey Shore or in Manhattan watching America's best fireworks with his parents, depending on how they were feeling that summer. They loved the fourth, and celebrating it without them still felt weird to him, especially now that he was making money off someone who shunned them. It dawned on Michael that this was the very first time he was spending the Fourth of July on Cape Cod, as Danny had never saw the need to invite him or his parents. "Death really does have a strange way of changing things," Michael said to himself in the otherwise empty room.

He walked the beach and took in the sights before heading back to the apartment to get ready for the big meeting. This big meeting may not have been discussing a nine figure sale, but he wanted to be on the top of his game. As the old saying goes, you can take the Big Apple broker out of the Big Apple, but you can't take the Big Apple out of the broker.

8

July 4

The first prospective buyer, Chris Bennett, owned a few bars and restaurants on Boston's South Shore. He told Michael he'd started off as a bartender in college, and it had just stuck. Chris was more than happy to spend a part of his holiday talking shop with Michael, and was eager to add another place to his web of successful food and drink spots. They talked financial figures for a while before Chris looked to change things up a bit.

"I say we take a food break. What's your favorite thing on the menu?"

"Well, I've never actually eaten the food here," Michael said, somewhat embarrassed.

"Seriously? You're missing out! This place has some of the best bar pizza in an area known for bar pizza," Chris said, not knowing if Michael was being sarcastic or not.

Michael was perplexed. As a New Yorker, he knew a thing or two about pizza, but 'bar pizza' was a foreign concept.

"What's so great about *bar* pizza?" he asked, as he was sure it came nowhere near the culinary beauty that was a real New York slice.

"The North Shore of Boston has the best roast beef sandwiches you'll ever have, and the South Shore ant to the same degree The Cape have bar pizza as their calling card."

"No way it compares to a New York slice though—I don't give a fuck how good you people think it is."

In the background, without so much as a prompt, Aubrey signalled to the cooks in the back to whip up a house pizza, not only so the negotiators could have some sustenance, but so the ever uptight Michael could have his South Shore bar pizza cherry popped in front of her. Her and Chris shared a wink that went unnoticed by Michael as soon as the pizza was rung in as if to quietly say, "We'll show him."

"By the way, Michael, I went to NYU so I do know a thing or two about New York Pizza," Chris subtly somewhat snarkily replied.

"I guess I stand corrected, then," Michael said as he sought to refocus the conversation on dollars and cents, rather than pies. It may seem un-American to change the topic, when the topic is pizza, but then again what is more American than a massive real estate/business sale?

Back on topic, Chris showcased his expertise in restaurant ownership. He also showed the battle scars he had accrued over many years working behind a bar. There isn't a bartender out there that hasn't sliced a finger while cutting fruit or gotten the nasty surprise that is hidden piece of glass. He said no matter how high he climbed, he still loved getting behind the bar to help a weeded bartender or running food to help beleaguered wait staff. Michael liked that quality, because it showed that just because someone's the boss doesn't mean they're above the common man. Michael may not have had the same quality, but when he saw it, he surely respected it.

Their conversation was interrupted when Aubrey placed that bar pizza in front of them and it was a sight to behold. In front of them was a crispy pie that was overflowing with cheese to the brim of the crust. Unlike every other pizza Michael had ever seen, there was no buffer zone between the end of the cheese and the end of the pie. The only thing stopping the cheese was, in fact, the very end of the pie. The toppings were a vision of culinary excellence-the pepperonis weren't tiny ones, they were the size of hockey pucks-and, like the cheese, also went right to the end of the pie.

"Holy fuck," Michael said as he burnt his mouth on his first bite of cheesy goodness "This is actually awesome."

"Better than a New York slice?" Aubrey asked. She couldn't help but laugh at his facial expressions.

Michael put the slice down and chugged a little before enlightening his audience with his take. "It's like this New York pizza is a bone-in filet steak-high end, cooked to perfection, and absolutely top of the line. This bar pizza is like a good old, American cheeseburger-same tree, different branch. More of a comfort food than something I'm going out of my way for, but amazing either way."

"Glad we turned you on to something you've been missing out on," Aubrey said with a bit of snark, as she took a break from ringing in another guest's order to weigh in on the not so secret negotiations taking place in front of her.

"If this deal gets done, I may have to give you a nice raise for assisting in getting this ball rolling," Chris said with a bit of smile as he gazed into the eyes of the somewhat amused current owner of the bar.

"You better hope I don't fire her first for neglecting the paying customers to eavesdrop on a monumental set of negotiations like this."

In the end, Michael got not only an education on how bar pizza was as much a part of Southeastern Massachusetts as hockey rinks and Steven Tyler sightings, but what he figured was a competitive first offer. He liked the way Chris ran his other restaurants, and his financial offer was more than solid. He also knew that only a sucker buys the first thing they see and that applies just as much to the seller's side of it. There were two months ahead to listen to offers, collect money from the bar and make his final decision-no need to rush the sale and give Chris the keys right away.

"Is all the food here that good?" Michael asked Aubrey in what must have been among the most unusual questions ever presented to her, the owner of a restaurant-who by this point had been around for a minute-asking her if the food at his restaurant was good. As Don King would say, "Only in America."

"Believe it or not, yes," Aubrey retorted, showing what she knew. "For a run of the mill, divey place, we've got some decent cuisine. What's that saying about books and their covers?"

"Don't judge a book by its cover. Judge it by the reviews other people leave online," Michael replied, sounding like true millennial.

"Speaking of online reviews, if you ever want a good laugh then read some of the web reviews about this place." Aubrey chimed in as over the years Danny's unsound techniques of running the place manifested themselves in ways that were apparent to the guests and those guests were good at letting it all be known on the internet.

"I can't say I have, but I am very intrigued," Michael said as he poured over some of the paperwork Chris had left him regarding a potential sale.

The night of Independence Day was much slower than its eve. The Whaler never sniffed the madness of the night before, and Michael didn't mind at all. The relative quiet gave him what he needed to thumb through review after review on his phone. What he quickly found was that each one was more kooky than the last. It was one thing to hear how screwed up his uncle was from the staff, but the customers were a different story. One guest wrote of a bartender being eviscerated in plain view of himself and his date by an "older, authoritarian man"-which didn't take Sherlock Holmes to deduce was Danny-for not leaving the bar to run food to a table while the place was fully staffed on a not-so-busy night. Another wrote of a "crotchety old man" screaming at a waitress for answering the restaurant's phone and committing the mortal sin of taking a to-go order. "NO TAKE OUT ON WEEKENDS, NO MATTER HOW SLOW IT IS!" read the all-caps direct quote, which said the outburst left the server feeling humiliated and the reviewer pledging never to return. To say Michael was perplexed as to how someone can so carelessly be a brute and alienate both staff and customers was the understatement of the century. But then again, that was Danny in a nutshell.

Aubrey, who by now was off the clock and enjoying a drink before heading out to watch the locals light up roman candles and call them a fireworks show, saw what he was reading, and offered her own two cents. "Not a whole lot of hyperbole going on in those reviews, by the way."

"Given what everyone's said about him, I figured no one was making anything up," Michael said as he put his phone down for the first time in what seemed like forever.

"He could be a royal prick, but being around him long enough helped me see his softer side," Aubrey said.

"Soft side? The guy was as soft as porcupine with a nail gun. What did that SOB do that was so soft?"

"A few years back a waitress, who was by no means a fan of his had a house fire and lost every worldly possession she ever had. Danny took all the sales from one of the busiest weekends of the summer and anonymously donated it to her, despite their mutual disdain for one another.

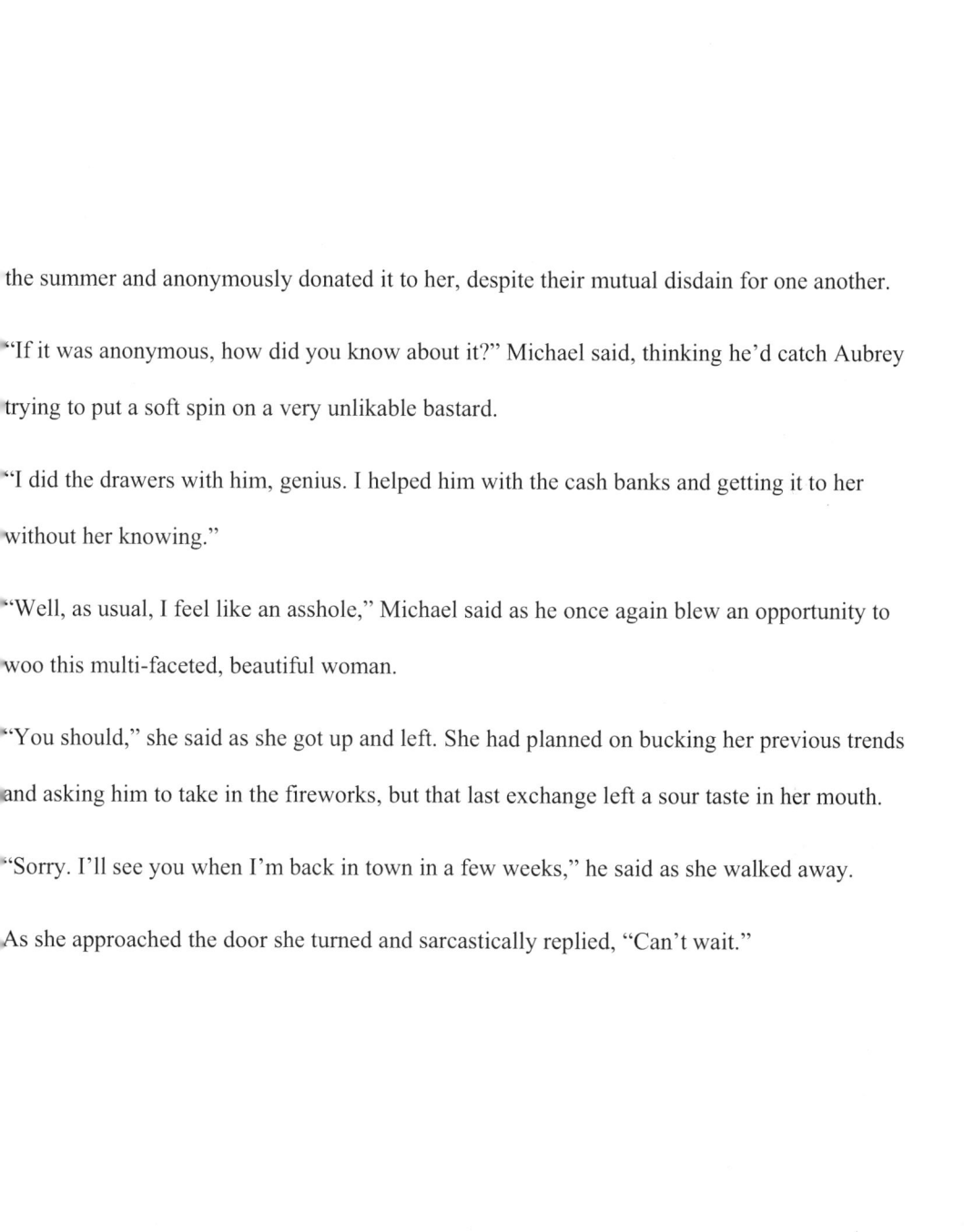

"If it was anonymous, how did you know about it?" Michael said, thinking he'd catch Aubrey trying to put a soft spin on a very unlikable bastard.

"I did the drawers with him, genius. I helped him with the cash banks and getting it to her without her knowing."

"Well, as usual, I feel like an asshole," Michael said as he once again blew an opportunity to woo this multi-faceted, beautiful woman.

"You should," she said as she got up and left. She had planned on bucking her previous trends and asking him to take in the fireworks, but that last exchange left a sour taste in her mouth.

"Sorry. I'll see you when I'm back in town in a few weeks," he said as she walked away.

As she approached the door she turned and sarcastically replied, "Can't wait."

9

July 16-17

After taking a few weekends away from the Cape, it was time to head up to spend a night in Provincetown with Nick and Brad. The happy couple were already in Provincetown, and would pick him up in Wellfleet. He figured that, while the neighborhood, it was worth checking in on the bar. They planned on meeting him in Wellfleet Saturday because he'd been so busy that week that he couldn't get out any earlier. This wasn't so bad, since he'd have a chance to check in on the bar before Nick picked him up and they headed up the Cape to Provincetown.

When Michael walked into the somewhat empty bar, he spied Colin using his phone on the clock, which in some places may have been a no go, but he really didn't care. He had much better things to do than get on a kid who was a good worker for checking out social media during some downtime. Colin saw Michael eying him while on his phone, and felt like the principal had just caught him red-handed. "I'll put it away right now," he said in a bit of a panic. "Sorry Michael."

"Don't worry about it. Answer me this though, what is it with you kids and your damn phones?" Michael asked Colin, knowing damn well he, too, spent an inordinate amount of time on his own phone and was coming off like a grumpy old man.

"I'm reading, so it's technically learning," Colin sarcastically fired back, feeling that whatever tension there was in the air had completely evaporated.

"Ernest Hemingway, I hope."

"Nope, Dave Portnoy. Nothing like reading Barstool Sports to take your mind off work for a hot second."

Michael couldn't help but laugh, since he, too, frequented the comedy site that masqueraded as a place for sports.

"He's a deviant, but I love his shtick. Big Cat, Jordie and Feits are all funny as hell too."

"It's a great place for some mindless entertainment. Viva." Colin finished as he put his phone away and got back to work cleaning glasses ahead of what would surely be a busy weekend.

As much as Michael would have loved to continue the locker room talk, he spied Aubrey and had to ask her the question that had been on his chest all week and something he was too scared to search on the internet.

"What's going on, stranger?" she asked and put a coaster down in front of him as she made her way towards the taps.

"I have kind of a weird question to ask, and I figured you'd be the person to go to," Michael said, knowing how much of an idiot he sounded like.

Aubrey stopped pouring a draft beer and paused in front of him. "I'm all ears. Hit me with your best shot."

He paused for a second, before locking eyes with Aubrey and with a bit of a stutter at first, asked, "What's up in Provincetown that everyone gets so damn excited about?"

She had a bit of a chuckle and she shook her head at Michael's naivety. "You really don't know, do you?"

"That's why I'm asking. Rule #1 in the Big Apple is never ask a question you already know the answer to. My co-worker is picking me up shortly to go up there for the weekend. "

"It's the gay capital of the Cape, and pretty much everywhere else. Don't ask me how it became that way; it just is."

"Oh boy," Michael said, as he realized his weekend was going to be a bit different than the "Cape weekends" he had become accustomed to.

"You're not a homophobe, are you?" Aubrey asked, not knowing if she was asking too a deep a personal question, but also knowing it was the 21st century.

"I live in New York City, which attracts them like a half off sale at Bloomingdales and the guy who invited me up there happens to be gay. Hell, I'm so pro-gay, I make Elton John look like Michele Bachmann."

"So you're using the 'I'm not racist, I have black friends' argument to show you're on Team Gay?" Aubrey replied as now she was almost full blown trolling him with not so subtle digs.

He was somewhat frustrated, but wouldn't let her see it. "No, I'm using the 'I live in the most diverse city in the world and have to do business with people of all walks of life' argument. You should look into it some time."

Knowing that despite her best efforts she had just been shut down with a vigorous retort all Aubrey could really do was put her tail between her legs and accept the loss she just took. "Anyway, have a good time up there."

"That's what I thought. I'll be sure to do just that," he said with a laugh as he headed out to wait for his ride outside.

As soon as Michael left the bar, Christina and Aubrey started laughing hysterically at the exact same moment. "Maybe a weekend with the gays will be good for him. I can't see his uppity act flying in P-Town," Christina said as she caught her breath between chuckles.

"Holy shit, can you imagine him sitting in a room of flamboyant gays? We think he's uptight as he is."

"Pray for Michael," Christina said as she gestured the sign of the cross before the duo went back to work.

Sure enough, at about 11:30 am the next morning, mere minutes after opening, Michael rolled in, clearly in some pain from the night before.

"Look like you need a coffee, a Bloody Mary, a gallon of water and about 15 aspirin," Aubrey said as he painfully pulled up a barstool in front of her.

"All of the above," Michael said as he cracked a smile through a hangover for the ages.

"I take it your night was as fun as your face is miserable right now," Aubrey said as she presented him a water and tried to determine exactly how urgent the need for the other three items was.

"My mom used to say 'gay nights make for sad mornings,' and while the context might have been a little bit different, she sure as hell was right. Goddamn, I had a great time last night," Michael said, as he inhaled his water like a camel in a desert oasis after six months in the Sahara.

"What exactly did you get yourself into?"

"Started out at the bar, so not too different than today. Did some bar-hopping, and eventually ended up at a house party on the beach. We had a bonfire, and it was damn near am when we called it a night."

"Sounds like you got the full Cape experience," Aubrey said as she put a hot cup of black coffee in front of him and started making the Bloody Mary she promised.

"I'll say. Being so close to the ocean really does have its perks."

Michael looked at the three cups in front of him and then looked up at Aubrey. "Three out of four promised items isn't too bad," he said referring to the absent aspirins.

"I'm not exactly a doctor, but something tells me that mixing painkillers and booze isn't exactly healthy for someone's insides. I kind of don't want you to die.

"Thanks Doctor Aubrey, any other health tips?" Michael asked as he took his first sip of the bloody. "Damn! Any mix with this vodka?"

"Wow. I thought New Yorkers could drink," Aubrey said, since she knew she was more than a little generous with her pour.

Michael looked defeated as he stared back at her. "Not the best look for New Yorkers. I'll have to atone for myself next weekend."

"Back to back weekends down here? We really should feel honored, I guess," Aubrey said as she refilled his water.

"You should," Michael said as he checked his phone for the time. His car was coming and he didn't want to run late for his flight.

"Is it gonna be another in, out, in and out again, like this weekend?" Aubrey asked.

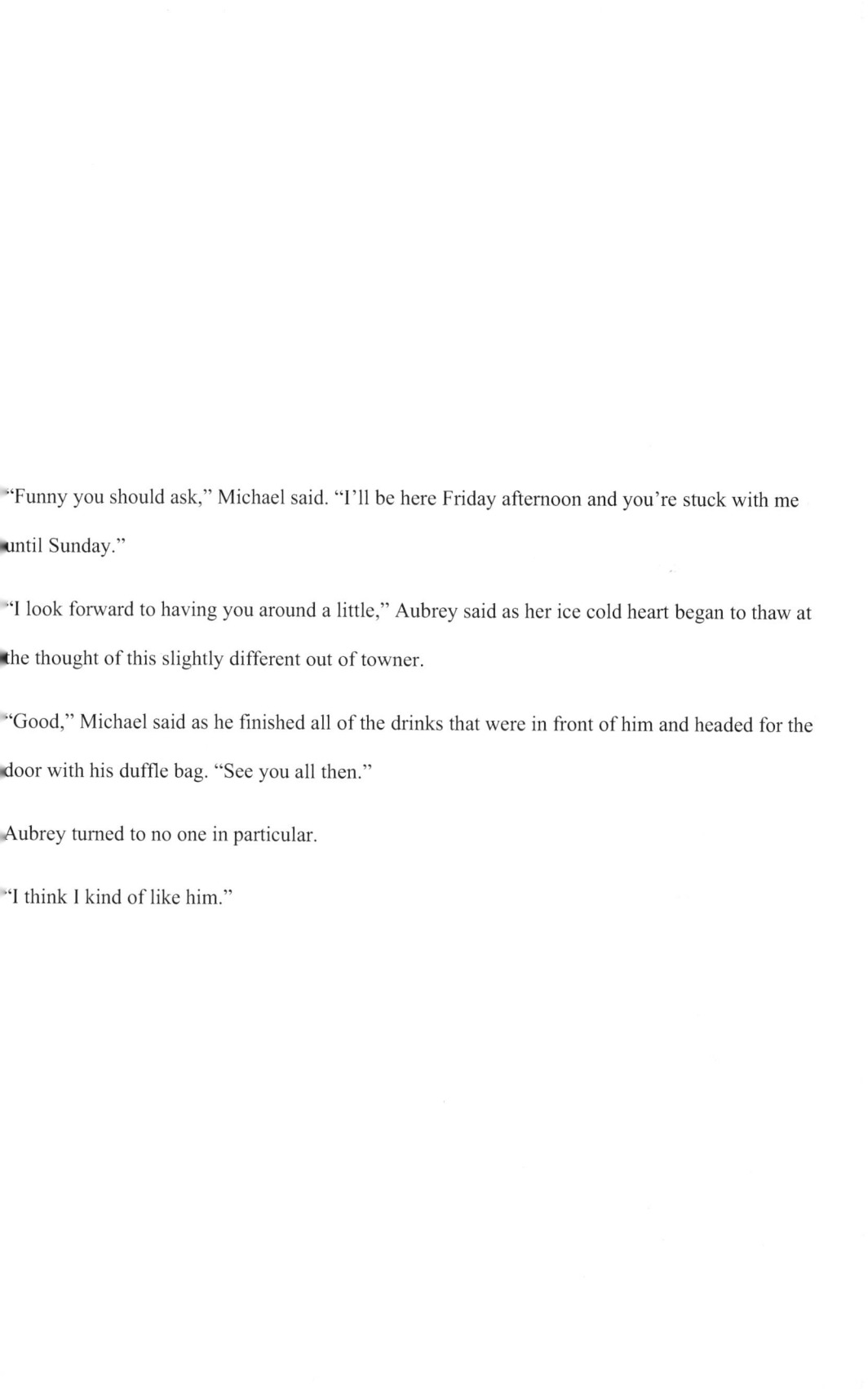

"Funny you should ask," Michael said. "I'll be here Friday afternoon and you're stuck with me until Sunday."

"I look forward to having you around a little," Aubrey said as her ice cold heart began to thaw at the thought of this slightly different out of towner.

"Good," Michael said as he finished all of the drinks that were in front of him and headed for the door with his duffle bag. "See you all then."

Aubrey turned to no one in particular.

"I think I kind of like him."

10

July 22

Michael had gotten used to arriving in town later on Friday nights, so being this early was an interesting little change up. He saw how the staff prepared for summer weekends, and how they recognized that getting out in front of a big push was the difference between staying in control and being overrun when it did get busy. He spied Colin coming in the front door in a polo shirt with a backpack and classic sunglasses tan lines. "Where are you coming from?" Michael asked.

"I scouted a Cape League matinee game today. Chatham was playing Orleans; ace pitcher for Orleans out of Miami is going top-five next June. Kid brought it today. "

"Ohio or Florida?" Michael somewhat sarcastically asked Colin, since two schools have Miami and University in their name, though only one goes by "Suntan U."

"The U," Colin replied, as he put up a half assed University of Miami double-hand gesture that is tied as tightly to the school in Coral Gables as sunshine and excellence on the football field.

"How'd Freddie Prinze Jr. do for Chatham?" Michael asked, assuming the reference to *Summer Catch* would go right over the young barback's head.

"Solid five innings before coming unraveled. There's a reason he got the boot from Framingham State. I got to sit next to Jessica Biel, though, she didn't so much as look at me, damn shame," Colin replied, showing his knowledge of the Cape League went beyond the field and into obscure early-2000s lousy sports movie references.

"I thought he was married to Sarah Michelle Gellar?" Christina chimed in as she swapped out the lunch menus behind the bar for dinner menus.

"It's from a movie, a damn good one at that," Colin told Christina quasi-sarcastically, as he transitioned from aspiring MLB scout to guy who cuts limes and restocks fridges.

"Oh, the baseball one they filmed down here? That piece of garbage sucked and gave the locals a bad name," Christina said as she got ready for the summer weekend evening push.

"Some people just don't appreciate great cinematography when they see it," Michael said, reassuring Colin that he was not alone in having a soft spot for shitty sports movies, especially after a night filled with a few libations.

After having himself a clam chowder and a cheeseburger, Michael held court at the bar and for the first time, went out of his way to interact with the locals. He may not have been planning to be around for long, but he was the boss and there was a certain way he felt he should act. Did his interactions with his guests come off as a little uppity? Sure, but in the eyes of his staff, it was some progress, and the place may just have been growing on him. He stayed in the bar until close, and even had an end-of-shift drink with his crew.

As they sat at the bar Aubrey, asked him the question she had been holding in for the all night. At almost 2 am, with a filthy shirt, her makeup ruined and her hair a mess, this was as good a time as any.

"What are you doing tomorrow during the day, boss?" she asked.

"Probably making sure you're not fucking anything up in here," Michael replied, with only the slightest hint of sarcasm.

"Well, you won't see me in here before 5 tomorrow, I've got the afternoon off and I'm going to the beach. I don't like swimming alone."

"Well, I guess I can audition for the role of a piece of chum in a *Jaws* remake," Michael said, while one of those smiles struck his face that only happens when you get a piece of really good news out of the clouds.

"11:30. Be there," Aubrey said as she headed for the door, knowing she had made his latest trip worth it.

"I'll have my best Speedo on," Michael replied, knowing damn well he'd be in a pair of Calvin Klein boardshorts that cost just a bit more.

As soon as Aubrey left the room, Colin chimed in like the immature kid in a room full of adults he still was. "I've been trying all summer, and you just come in from Manhattan and get her?"

As much as he wanted to slap the little bastard, Michael remembered that at 22, he probably would have said something similar. He took a deep breath and tried to make this a teaching moment. "I don't *have* her. We're friends, and I happen to be her boss."

Apparently Colin's recently completed four years of college quenched his thirst for knowledge and he offered yet another sarcastic reply. "Be real, Dude, she invited you to the beach and clearly likes you. Must be great to be the boss and have a shitload of money."

Rather than lose his patience, Michael pretty much just played along with the youngster, because there was a better chance of Christ coming down off the cross, turning on the faucet and making tap water into cabernet than a real heart-to-heart happening. "Well, when you have a job that doesn't require you to have a filthy shirt and carry cases of beer upstairs all night then I'm sure the ladies will be tripping over each other to get to you."

"So what you're saying is when I become the next Billy Beane, I'll be a ladies man, to boot,"

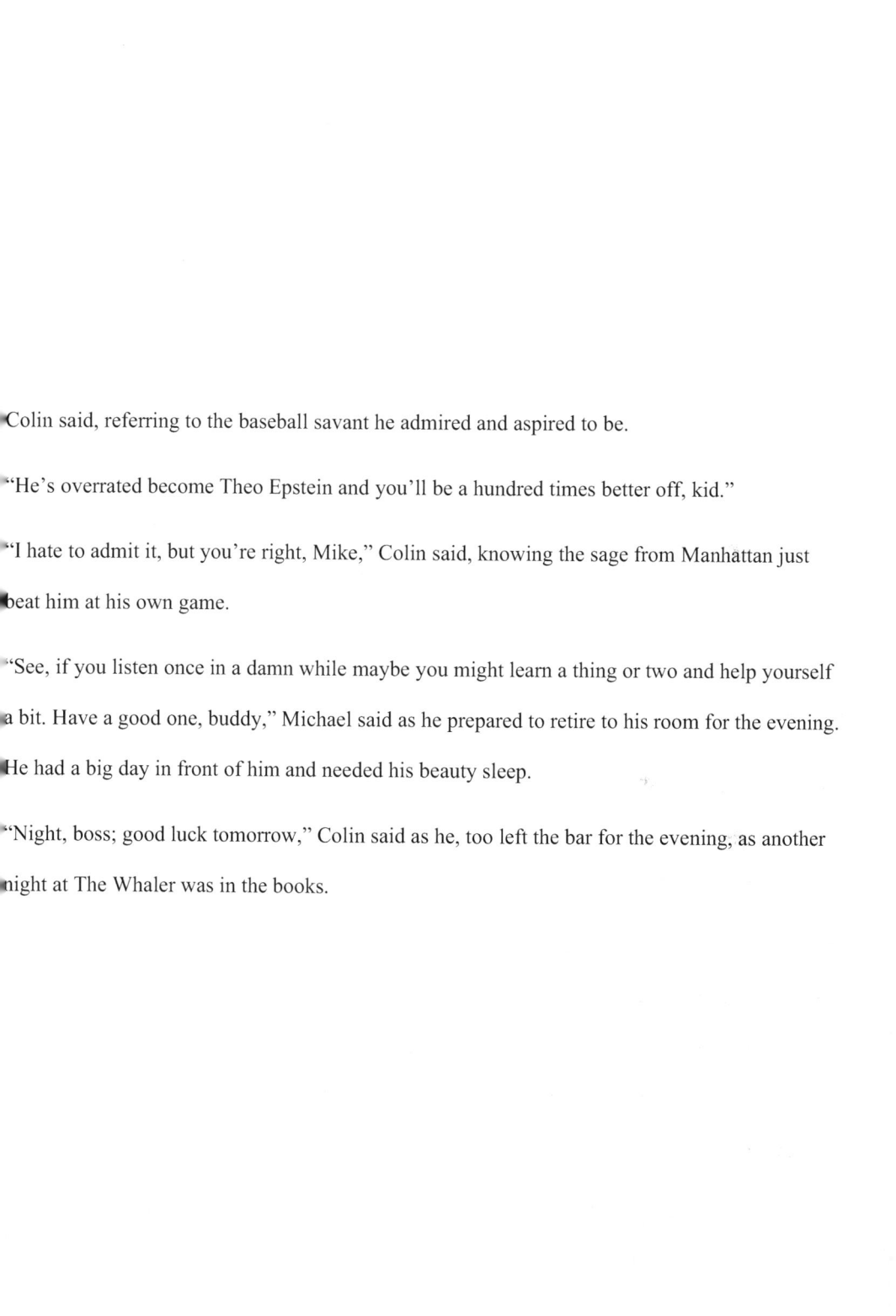

Colin said, referring to the baseball savant he admired and aspired to be.

"He's overrated become Theo Epstein and you'll be a hundred times better off, kid."

"I hate to admit it, but you're right, Mike," Colin said, knowing the sage from Manhattan just beat him at his own game.

"See, if you listen once in a damn while maybe you might learn a thing or two and help yourself a bit. Have a good one, buddy," Michael said as he prepared to retire to his room for the evening. He had a big day in front of him and needed his beauty sleep.

"Night, boss; good luck tomorrow," Colin said as he, too left the bar for the evening, as another night at The Whaler was in the books.

11

July 23

For a city slicker, Michael wasn't a bad swimmer. Spending a few summers on the Jersey Shore helped him understand the ocean and how it was an entirely different animal than a YMCA pool. That understanding was at the forefront of Michael's head as he stood eye to eye with Aubrey, waist deep in the ocean.

"How bad is the rip tide here?" he asked, as there had been a little bit of an awkward silence as they greeted each other and decided to take a dip rather than lay on a towel on this hot summer day.

"Oh, it's bad, and if does drag you out, there's a better than zero chance there's a great white out there waiting for you," Aubrey said with only a slight hint of hyperbole. "Those things can't tell the difference between stock brokers and harbor seals, either."

"Don't want that to happen-that kinda shit could ruin your whole week," Michael said coolly as he was now kind of on the lookout for fins.

"If you do get caught in a riptide, don't panic and swim against it. Let it take you, and swim perpendicular to it. That's how you get out of one with your life," Aubrey said, revealing a shocking amount of nautical knowledge.

"So it's like falling in love," Michael said, as he revealed his philosophical side.

"How do you figure?"

"It's easy to try to and fight it, but fighting it is the easiest recipe for getting hurt. Go with it, let it take you, and you'll almost always end up perfectly fine," Michael said, shocking himself with his ability to connect drowning in a riptide with the beautifully abstract concept of falling in love.

"So, Plato, do you want to take this conversation on to the shore? I want to get a little tan and I'm not trying to fall in love with any riptides-not today, anyway."

"You got it," Michael replied, as he knew as he was safe from shark attacks on the shore. Aubrey was a different story, since at this time of year, coastal towns throughout New England become infested with land sharks.

"How well did you know your Uncle Danny?" Aubrey asked him as the two walked from the shoreline and into the beach's rolling dunes.

"Well, I didn't really. Mom and him never really got along, and my Dad completely despised him, so, outside of a trip up here after my grandmother died when I was 10, I don't think I ever really spoke to him," Michael said, as he knew explaining the complexities of his family relationships was opening up a can of worms even the biggest cynics wouldn't touch with a 12-foot pole.

"You were up here as a kid?" she asked. "What was that like?"

"Yep," Michael began, as his brain went into overdrive trying to think up any and all details of that weekend over two decades earlier. "My mom and him reconnected at my grandmother's funeral and they decided a 'family weekend' up here would be a good for everyone. The first night was good, I guess, but the second night we were here we were at The Whaler having dinner-the four of us-my parents, Danny and I-and Danny screamed at a waitress for not putting the Shirley Temple I was drinking on our bill. That set off a powder keg because my mother thought he was acting like an ass, and after some insults both ways, we were back in Jersey first thing the next morning."

Aubrey couldn't help herself but have a chuckle, because *she* had been on the receiving end of Danny's verbal whiplash countless times over matters that anyone else would label innocuous. "That sounds like Danny. Always having to do it his way, regardless of who it hurt or alienated."

"Yep. That was the last time he spoke to my parents or myself. He didn't go to either of their funerals, so I saw no reason to make the trip up here when he kicked the bucket earlier this year," Michael said, as he realized how truly fucked up his family dynamic truly was as it's one thing to think it to yourself, but another view entirely to actually verbalize it to someone else.

The whole time they were on the beach and in the water, Michael wanted to ask her what brought the change of heart, but there just was never really an opening and why fuck up a good thing, he thought to himself. While they were laying on the now overly sandy towel, Aubrey caught Michael checking his phone. "What's going on in that walled-up street in New York that's more important than this?"

He couldn't help but laugh at her when he gave her an answer she wasn't expecting "I was just checking in on my Yankees. Big one up in Toronto, Sabathia on the bump."

"I'd tell you the Yankees suck, but your Danny would have gone into a tirade about how much Toronto sucks. Nothing but disdain for that city from him."

"What did he have against Toronto?" Michael asked as he had been to the sprawling Ontario metropolis a few times and really had nothing but great things to say.

"You didn't know?"

"Know what?"

"Wow," Aubrey began. "Your uncle had a tryout with the Toronto Maple Leafs back in the '70s, and according to him, looked pretty damn good out there. He was hazed nonstop for being an American, and eventually (and in his eyes, unfairly) was sent to the minor leagues. He was so pissed, he swore off hockey for good right then and there, and carried it around like an anchor for the rest of his life."

At that moment on that stretch of sand in New England, so much about Michael's past started to make sense as a few loose ends were tied up. "So that's where his misery began?" he asked.

"Oh yeah. He became miserable in general, but anything that reminded him of that failed tryout in Toronto was especially painful for him. Hockey, anything Canadian, hell I'm sure if he could have run a bar without any ice, he would have. I can't tell you how many times I had to hold back laughter when a guest ordered a Molson or Canadian Club."

Michael laughed at her sarcasm, but quickly realized she wasn't kidding. Danny's hockey career going down like the Titanic with a little less ice caused him to push everyone who loved him away. Hockey was his passion, and it more or less fucked him over. So in turn, he wouldn't let anyone get too closed to him, because they could screw him over as well. In his little ocean side impromptu psychological evaluation of his late uncle Michael realized quickly that while he couldn't condone the way Danny treated others-including Michael and his parents-there was a reason why he was the way he was. "Thank you," he said to Aubrey.

"For what?"

"For helping me understand the whole dynamic and, in a weird way, closure," Michael said as he shook his head.

"You're welcome," she said, as she leaned in, and casually popped the first-kiss cherry. The smiles on both of their faces told the whole story of how special of a moment this was.

A few more minutes would pass with giggles, like a pair of high school kids sneaking out for the first time, being the extent of their communication. Then reality set in that it was getting late. and The impromptu love fest on the beach would have to come to an end. "Shit," Aubrey said. "If we don't get out of here now, I'll be late, and I don't think my boss will be happy."

"I'll talk to him and see if he lets this one slide," Michael said with an ear to ear shit eating grin.

"Thank God. I'll try to save you a seat as a symbol of my never ending gratitude," Aubrey said, as she headed towards her car to head to the bar. She may have been "just a bartender" but she took her work very seriously and it would be a cold day in hell before she no-showed on a Saturday night, no matter who she was falling head over heels for.

As he sat on his stool at the borderline overcrowded bar, Michael heard a commotion brewing behind him and turned around to get a look. By the time his head spun around, the first punch had been thrown, and as the owner he felt it was his duty to break up the nonsense and lay down the law. This was easier said than done once one of the combatants-a youngster dressed in designer plaid shorts-smashed a beer bottle over a table and was ready to do some damage to his much-older opponent. Michael was in no rush to charge at the now armed walking epitome of a douchebag, as this was not the hill he wanted to die on. Luckily for him, a pair of guys, both much tougher than him-Brendan and Joey, the door guy-came right in and tackled the kid. As they brought him to the ground and his opponent tried to get in a revenge cheap shot, Michael shouted, "Get the fuck out of here, and if I see you in here again, I'm filing a goddamned restraining order."

The threat, coupled with the youngster being dragged out the door by the local duo brought a swift end to what could have been a very ugly scene. It was 12:30 am, and while there was technically another half hour until close, Michael gave the signal to turn the lights on-this Saturday night was over. The patrons weren't exactly thrilled, but they could see why he'd be shutting down early-nothing good could come of another 30 minutes of booze flowing.

Once the dust settled Michael realize his hand was bleeding, as one of the shards of glass must've nicked him and it was more than the paper cuts he was used to.

"Fuck. This'll need stitches," he said, as he realized going to the emergency room would throw a real wrench in his plans of catching the first flight out in the morning.

"Let me take a look," Aubrey said, as she gently looked at as his hand and walked him towards the back where the first aid kit was. When they got to the first aid kit, Michael took a seat on an upside down bucket as Aubrey emptied the kit and began an impromptu surgery.

She wouldn't be mistaken for Florence Nightingale anytime soon, but she realized that, as bad as the cut looked, if she could get the bleeding to clot, then Michael could avoid the ER and be back in Manhattan on time. A lot of rubbing alcohol, some liquid bandage, gauze, and plenty of tape seemed to do the trick. "Change the wrapping when you get home tomorrow and keep it covered for the next couple of days," she said as she finished.

"Where does a bartender with a business degree learn how to take care of a bad cut like that?" Michael asked.

"Five summers of lifeguarding on Humarock Beach taught me something other than how to hide vodka and orange juice in a water bottle. Never thought I'd ever actually get to put it to use," Aubrey said, as she realized how stupid that must've sounded. There's a bit of a dropoff between sitting in a swimsuit all day and being a real medical professional.

"You must've been a vision in your lifeguard uniform," Michael said as his sense of humor clearly hadn't taken the same blow his hand had.

Aubrey couldn't help but laugh at his ability to find something funny a few minutes after having his hand sliced open. The two were in the middle of a "moment," when Brendan came into the kitchen somewhat out of breath. Michael looked up at him and was beyond gracious for his actions.

"Dude, you saved my life back there," said Michael. "Thanks, bro."

"No worries. That little punk is everything that's wrong with this generation. How's the hand treating you?"

"You know. Lonely nights might be a little lonelier for the next few weeks, but beyond that, just glad it's not any worse. What started that whole thing?"

"I wonder why he'd have such lonely nights," Aubrey sarcastically mumbled while the boys continued to talk over her.

"Kid mouthed off to the guy. Then when cornered, he reached for something, like a typical entitled little asshole. Cops were outside and took them both in. I left out the bottle part. They'll both get drunk and disorderly charges and be out on Monday morning."

"Shit. Who called the police?" Michael asked. The last thing he wanted was this place to be the

East Coast's own Roadhouse.

"Some chick inside who's dating a cop," Brendan began. "This sort of shit happens a few times per summer. Comes with the territory down here this time of year."

"So it won't be a big deal?"

"God no. Think about being a cop down here-they have a few months of dealing with drunken assholes, and then nothing during the offseason. Gotta get the action in while you can."

"Either way, I'm appreciative. Help yourself to the Buds in the cooler," Michael said as he realized a few cold ones was the best and most thoughtful way to thank Brendan for being Johnny on the Spot.

"I'll take you up on that. But I have another favor to ask. Can we get down to business on me possibly buying The Whaler? I'm not using this as leverage, but I just want to get the ball rolling."

"I'm back in town next weekend. We'll set something up, and see if we can't hammer out a deal," Michael said, as he realized he'd have to at least listen to the bar fly's pitch on why he should be the one to buy the place he drinks in.

"You got it. Now I'm going to raid the Budweiser cooler like a goddamned green beret, if you don't mind."

"Have at it, Hoss," Michael said. Without Brendan, his busted hand would be a helluva lot worse.

"Punk kids coming in and causing trouble. Some things never change around here," Aubrey said as she stared into Michael's now bloodshot eyes.

"The kids were probably from Toronto. Nothing good ever stems from there," Michael joked.

Aubrey couldn't help but laugh at the subtle dig at Danny.

"You're such a dick. But somehow, you pull it off, so, congrats."

"Thanks. It's a skill, really."

"Cleaning a bar is a skill, too, and we can't get out of here until it's tidied up, so let's go," Aubrey said, as she led Michael from the kitchen into the bar area and was pleasantly surprised.

While they had been chatting/performing triage, Colin and David-with the help of a Budweiser wielding Brendan-had done most of the work, and all that really needed to done was counting and divvying up the tips.

"Hey, Boss do you any good chiropractors in New York City?" Colin yelled across the room to Michael.

"I'm sure there's one or two in the Tri-State NYC area. Why?"

"Because my back hurts from carrying this fucking place so much," Colin replied.

"One more word out of you, and your mouth is gonna hurt, too," Michael began, before pausing. "Once my hand heals up."

"They should give you a Purple Heart or some sort of medal because you took a helluva hit out there," Colin said as dramatically acted out taking a big hit in the head.

"I'll settle for getting out of here at a reasonable hour. So get back to work."

"You got it, bossman," Colin replied as he finished stocking the cooler and waited for his tipout for a night of hard work.

When the final tips were spread out, Christina-who was taking care of the drawers and making sure the alarm system was activated-David, Colin, and Brendan-who was now on his fifth free Budweiser-took the collective hint and scurried out the door, leaving the "couple of the hour" alone in the bar. They chit-chatted for about 20 minutes as Michael danced around the burning question, he realized it was pretty much now or never.

"Do you want to come upstairs?" he asked Aubrey, point blank, without sounding like too much of a dickhead, which he'd admit wasn't always easy.

"I thought you were gonna spend all night dancing with your hand on my ass without making your move," Aubrey replied, trying to be as veiled and hard to get as possible.

"So, is that a yes?" Michael asked, not totally sure of where she was going with her philosophical diatribe.

"It is. Let's fucking go," Aubrey replied as she grabbed her purse and headed for the side stairs with Michael already leading the way.

Michael had been bloodied and bruised and was going to have explain his busted up hand to his white-collar coworkers, but at the end of the day, he got the girl. There isn't a red-blooded man from Wellfleet to Washington State that wouldn't take that deal every single time.

"Why don't you just let me drive you to the airport? I'm free all day and my car is downstairs.," Aubrey said as she laid in bed while Michael got his stuff together for the trip back to the Big Apple.

"I told you, I already have the black car paid for and I don't want to be a burden," Michael replied as he scoured the apartment, looking for anything he didn't want to leave behind.

"Take the boy out of Manhattan, but you can't take the Manhattan out of the boy, even though he's from Jersey," Aubrey said trying to push Michael's buttons.

He stopped dead in his tracks and with a plain face that may or may not have been facial sarcasm just looked Aubrey dead in the eyes.

"Don't bring that up. I'm Manhattan through and through honey."

"You got it, Jersey Boy," Aubrey said, not sure how he'd reply.

He didn't reply at all, at least not verbally, as he climbed back into bed with her and gave her a kiss. Her sass would have rubbed plenty of people the wrong way, but not Michael. He was far too smitten to get upset over such innocuous shit.

"Hey, so, before I go, what exactly are we? Like, status-wise?" There was plenty of mutual affection, but given the distance and other mitigating factors, he had trouble coming up with a word for their type of "relationship".

"I'm not sure and I don't want to ruin it by putting a label on it just yet, so let's just see where it goes," Aubrey said. "I really like you, though." She too struggled to come up with a word to call what they were, but was open about the affection.

"That feeling is 100 percent mutual."

"Good. I was beginning to think you were just after me for my money," Aubrey said with a wry smile.

"Hey, that's my line."

"You've got to be quick to keep up with me," she replied with a smile. "You'll learn that on the fly-I hope, anyway. Otherwise, I may just leave you in the dust with my beauty and wit."

Michael already learned that looks were deceiving with Aubrey and he was coming to realize that she was a much deeper book than even he imagined.

"You can leave me anywhere you want, just don't leave me there alone." The car was pulling up to the front of the bar and as much as Michael wanted to stick around he had to go to New York where a pile of work was waiting for him on the other side.

"Well, I'll see you next week. Can't leave you alone up here," Aubrey said as she planted one last kiss on his lips and walked him out the door. The two had one last mini-makeout session as Michael opened the car door. "Be safe. Text me when you get back to the City."

"Will do," he said as he as he slid into the car. He waved as he pulled away, and like a child going away on a road trip, his head jerked around, looking at where he came from, so he wanted to capture one last glimpse of her before it was back to reality. He'd be back and she'd be waiting for him, but he wondered how long this arrangement could keep. He decided that everything ends at some point, and rather than focus on the inevitable end of what he had with Aubrey, he should savor what they had and enjoy it, because such mutual passion isn't easy to find. They didn't have a label for what they had-in fact, labelling something so special and so unique as what they felt for each other would be selling it short.

12

July 25-30

That week at work was one giant drag, which working in the summer in the City almost always was. Not only was the market a little bit slower during the summer, but the oppressive heat and humidity turned the concrete jungle into the damn Amazon, but with different types of wild animals roaming around. Sitting in his air-conditioned office, Michael was secretly longing for the ocean breezes and slightly more laid back way of life with his new "love interest," but this was his reality, and from Monday to Friday, 9-5, Cape Cod may damn well have been in a galaxy far, far away. It only took about an hour after he got to his desk on Monday morning for the first person to ask about his injury as Brianna, a young broker, who not too long ago was a sorority girl at the University of Wisconsin asked "What the fuck happened to you?"

A few months earlier, maybe he would have been extra defensive—and to a certain degree, ashamed of himself—for being in such a lowly place, but Michael answered most proudly "Had to take a stand against a guy acting out in my bar."

"Bar room brawl for a guy like you?" Brianna fired back as this was a different Michael than she had grown used to working with during their time together at the NYSE.

"It's the cost of doing business sometimes," he answered as her silent judgements were rolling off him.

"You would have fit in great in Madison back in the day. Seemed like a massive fight stemming from a frat boy being overserved was a weekly rite of passage."

"Believe it or not, I spent most college weekends in my dorm studying to get ahead for the week, it's why I have this job." Michael said, knowing damn well that despite his dedication to bookwork he did have his fair share of fun.

"Right, I'm sure you were President of the Temperance movement at Columbia," she as she walked away and back to her cube.

As soon as she left Michael took a long look at his injured finger and thought about the crazy last few months aloud. "If only she knew."

Five days back in the city shockingly flew by, and by Friday afternoon, it was back to Cape Cod for Michael. Like clockwork, he took an early evening flight out of LaGuardia, had a livery pick him up at the airport and he was in Wellfleet just after the first real rush of the evening arrived. On this Friday night the crowd was lively, and everyone seemed more interested in having a good time than having any fisticuffs, which, after earlier events, was more than fine for him. Aubrey was clearly busy, but she took the second to give him a kiss over the bar when she first saw him, as the two didn't care what anyone thought about their PDA. "Bar kisses," as the duo quickly labelled it, were yet another facet of the still unnamed bond they shared. The night went by smoothly, and Michael was really able to kick back and enjoy the atmosphere of the place. With every sip of beer to his lips, the thought of work went further and further away.

At the end of the night, he sat there as his employees cleaned the bar and counted the better-than-average amount of money they had made, when Christina gave him a rude awakening.

"You have a meeting with Brendan tomorrow at his place at 11:30 am. I took the liberty of setting it up for you."

"Shit, I forgot all about that," Michael remarked, as he quickly remembered this was, at least in some regards, a business trip.

"Don't worry about it, I'll drive you over and pick you up afterwards. Least I can do, boss," Christina replied, much to his relief.

"Thank you, I really appreciate it."

"Considering the negotiations could very well determine whether or not I still have a job, I'm more than happy to play the role of chauffeur. Besides, if I don't, Aubrey will have to, and there won't be an am bartender, and anarchy will ensue."

"We can't have that," Michael said as he gave Aubrey a look that said 'I want you,' without saying anything.

"Anarchy in a bar is something we try to avoid," Aubrey said, as she jumped into the conversation. "Other forms of anarchy aren't so bad, though." She bobbed her chin the door, showing Michael she was just as adept at nonverbal cues.

"Have a good one, guys. I'll see everyone tomorrow," Michael said as he and Aubrey exited stage right to retire to the apartment for the night.

As they were heading for the door, Christina issued a bold warning to the pair of love birds.

"I don't care what the two of you do to each other tonight and I really would rather not know, but just make sure you're at work on time, and he's ready to go at 11 AM. If I have to go up there and break up a Saturday morning spooning, so help me, fucking god."

"Done and done," Aubrey said, as she was whisked out the door and up the stairs.

Michael was more than happy to bum a ride from Christina to Brendan's for their big "negotiation," since getting around in this neck of the woods was anything but his forte. On the ride out to Brendan's house, all Michael could imagine was some ramshackle cottage in the dunes that looked more like a shack than a home, and at first glance, that's all it was. Then he looked to the right of the "shack," and realized the chic-looking home was where Brendan lived. As Michael knocked on the door, he couldn't help but be impressed. "Brendan the electrician lives *here*?" he said, just loud enough for Christina to hear.

"Yup, he's far from a working class stiff," Christina replied. "He knows a thing or two about how to make money, and make it last."

"I'll say," said Michael as he got out of the car and headed towards Brendan's freshly painted white door.

When Brendan opened up the door Michael was even more amazed, as the place had all the amenities of his bachelor pad in Manhattan with a slightly more picturesque view-though he'd never admit that. In fact, Brendan's place looked more like a vacation home than a place a single, middle aged blue collar worker lived twelve months a year.

"I thought you'd never show. I figured if a meeting was going down anywhere, except in a boardroom, it was below your first world standards," Brendan said as he cracked open his stainless steel refrigerator. "Can I get you a beer?"

"I guess I can stomach a Budweiser, if that's what you've got," Michael said knowing he'd damn well rather drink his own piss than the pride of St. Louis.

"Are you kidding? What kind of host would I be if I didn't cater to my audience? Here's a Corona for you; hell, I'll even throw in a lime. I know how you one percenters can get when things aren't perfect," Brendan said as he handed Michael the beer, lime and all. "It's on the house, or to put it in language a New Yorker would understand, $10 less than you'd pay in Manhattan."

"Thanks. I'm not literally a one percenter, I'm still working my ass to get to that tax bracket. Do you have people up here often?" Michael said as he admired the view of the dunes and little glimmer of ocean he could see over top of them.

Brendan couldn't help, but laugh. "What do you think, that I'm some sort of fucking hermit that goes to work then goes home and lives in total isolation from everyone? Just because I'm not the most social butterfly at the bar doesn't mean I can't court company. I own a house on the beach, who wouldn't want to come up here?"

"I misread the book that you are, Brendan, and for that for that, I'm sorry," Michael said, as he pressed his beer to his lips and pulled up a seat at Brendan's dining room table that had more paperwork on it than a dorm room during 'cram for finals' time.

"Before we get down to it, I have to compliment you on that picture. He's one hell of a player," Michael said, pointing across the room to a framed and autographed shot of NHLer Charlie Coyle that was hung on the wall the way a family would have a pic of a trip to Disney.

"Thanks! I wired his sister's yoga studio last year, and got that as a perk-he's a nice kid. Gets me tickets when he's playing up in Boston to play the Bs. He told me if his team ever wins the Stanley Cup, I'm invited to the party and can drink as much I want; I just have to wire the dance floor for it."

"Sounds like a helluva deal, hopefully he gets it done-just not before my Rangers. Let's go to work-hit me with what you got," Michael said as the inner broker in him came out the mood went from something as light-hearted as a local hockey player to how this seven figure transaction would go down.

The two poured over the countless documents that Brendan had laid out, and it quickly dawned on Michael that, for a guy with a lot less "business education" than he had, this blue collar guy knew his stuff, and documented *everything*. All the years of doing electrical work across Massachusetts without spending money for the sake of spending it nor going down the wife and kids rabbit hole meant his back account was far from skimpy and with a *little* help from the local bank, he could afford the transaction, especially with the terms he had in mind.

What Brendan proposed was buying the property and the liquor license entirely, while keeping Christina in charge of the day to day operations-albeit with a slight raise-as she clearly knew what she was doing. The company itself would be 90 percent Brendan's, but Michael would be kept on as a minority owner, with the remaining 10 percent, and essentially, as Brendan put it, pocket a nice piece of the summer profits without assuming much risk. It wasn't the all-out, cash-out that Michael was looking for, but it would be a nice chunk of change up front, and the ability to have a stake in the bar long term would mean more money coming in annually. Before Michael left to ponder the offer, Brendan sweetened the pot by saying an old plumber friend of his had extensive knowledge of revamping aging septic systems, and that he'd have him do the work if Michael sold him the place.

Michael didn't so much as have to ask a question as Brendan was out in front on every facet of a potential sale. Hi offer was solid, and it would allow Michael the opportunity to make more money in the long-term with next to no risk by keeping a small stake in the bar. It wasn't so much that he got sentimental all of a sudden, but he did have a soft spot for the people that worked there-especially Aubrey-and the chance to be around here even on a very part time basis, was more than enough reason to at least consider it.

When Michael walked into the bar following his meeting Aubrey was patiently waiting for him as she had gotten off her shift and took up residence on a barstool. After having a kiss, she sat back and looked at him. "Is Brendan gonna be the new head honcho now?"

"That information is classified, if I told you I'd have to kill you," Michael said with a smile.

"So tell me."

"Never," Michael said as he kept the playful banter going.

"C'mon, if you don't just tell me you know I have my ways of getting it out of you," Aubrey said as her "ruthlessness" knew no bounds.

When faced with the reality of not getting any Michael put it out there. "He made a really great offer that would keep me on as a minority owner and I'm weighing the option. I still want to have one more meeting with another potential buyer, but I can see myself taking this deal."

Aubrey's secret desire to get a 9-5 and leave the industry had been on her mind all summer, so much so that she had been looking at job postings around the internet. Michael taking Brendan's deal could complicate that, but she never tipped her hand either way. "I hope you do," she answered with a smile.

13

August 3

Michael's work day had been over for about an hour, but he was still at his desk and was really in no rush to head home. While he knew staying after would earn him brownie points with his higher ups, he was also in the midst of a day-long textual conversation with Aubrey that had become a big part of his daily routine and he was in no rush to end it. Selfies, funny stories, and everything else were exchanged and while there may have been some distance between them the beauty that is technology alleviated at least some of that. When Michael was thinking about heading for the door he felt a tap on his shoulder and turned to see Patrick Larkin, an older broker, who was more of an acquaintance than a close friend standing there.

"What's going on Pat?" Michael asked as he gestured like he was heading out the door.

"Not too much. Do you have a second?" Patrick replied.

"Sure."

"Have you sold that pub in Massachusetts yet?"

"How did you even know I owned and was looking to sell a bar?" Michael replied as he hadn't said more than a dozen words to this guy in the past year.

"Word gets around. People talk."

"Well, I haven't sold it. Yet."

"Good," Patrick said gleefully. "If you want I know a potential buyer from up there that's got some pretty deep pockets."

"Who?"

"Martin Williams, he's really into the real estate scene in Massachusetts and he's looking to break into the food and beverage world."

Michael was intrigued, "How do you know this guy?"

"We were fraternity brothers in college and we caught up at our reunion in Boston this past weekend. He's always looking for property on Cape Cod and I mentioned your name and situation."

While Michael wasn't looking for Patrick to be his agent, he did appreciate him accidently bringing him another potential offer-which would bring the bidders to three. If this guy was as Patrick said he was then a potential deal could be done just in time for Labor Day. "Send him my information and we'll talk."

"Will do," Patrick said as he began to leave Michael's desk.

"One more thing," Michael said before Patrick could get too far away, "how much commission are you bringing in on this?"

Patrick laughed, "Let's just say not enough. Maybe he'll throw me a round if he buys the place."

"Good man," Michael said as now it was time to go home and maybe get a FaceTime with Aubrey if she was up for it.

14

August 26-28

It was a rainy, August Friday when Michael walked into a boardroom in Boston's Seaport to meet with Martin Williams. This time around, he flew right from New York to Boston and would head to the Cape from the Hub. He was still very much intrigued by the thought of selling the bar to Brendan and keeping a toe in the water, but all he ever heard Martin was that he had deep pockets and he lusted for buying real estate the way your average red blooded man would lust over Angelina Jolie.

"Martin Williams-you can call me Marty," the well-dressed real estate mogul said, as he held out his right hand and borderline obnoxiously put his left on Michael's shoulder.

"Michael O'Reilly-call me Michael."

"You're a funny one," Marty said in an uppity and, once again, completely obnoxious manner that bordered on nauseating, even for a guy like Michael, who spent his life around such people on Wall Street.

"I try," Michael replied as he just wanted to get down to business and get away from this blowhard as quickly as possible, preferably with some of his coin in his bank account.

Before they got down to crunching numbers and setting the parameters for a deal, Marty Williams had to show Michael the pictures of his family on his phone. Appeasing a buyer or seller by exchanging personal bullshit was nothing new to him, but this guy might as well have been in the Hall of Fame of WASPY asshole-ism. His daughter was a sophomore field hockey player at Stonehill College in Massachusetts and his son-his pride and joy-was a senior football captain at the ever unlikable Boston College High School. Michael worked hard to control his laughs, and quite frankly, he should have won an Oscar for acting like he gave a shit about this potential buyer's two kids.

"She's a future Stepford Wife masquerading as a college athlete, and he might as well be a Lands' End model who plays high school ball on the side," Michael thought, while he was subjected to torture he was sure was illegal under the Geneva Convention. "Lovely family," was all he could come up with as he watched the clock and wanted to get down to business like never before, but getting in a word in edgewise to get the proceedings going took effort and more than a little patience.

When Marty Williams wasn't jabbering on and on about the exploits of his offspring, he was sharing his love of his alma mater, Boston College, as though he'd gone to an Ivy. After he wrapped up his spiel about BC, he turned to Michael and asked, "Where'd you graduate from?" in a manner that suggested the response would be a SUNY school or the like.

"Undergrad at Columbia. MBA at Penn," he quickly replied with a hint of pretention to remind Mr. Williams that his alma mater wasn't the most impressive at the table. If this WASP wanted to have a dick measuring contest, he better damn well know he was up against a bona fide, hall of fame cocksman.

"Impressive. Let's get to work, shall we?" Marty said as he felt slightly defeated by this younger, more attractive out-of-towner. For a man who was so used to being the smartest guy in every room and being fawned over this was a slight change of pace.

When they began going over the details of the potential sale, Michael was impressed at not only how much Marty was offering-a bit more than Brendan's offer-but how much he wanted this place. Michael was a bit concerned about what would happen to the bar, as he heard the Williams family had a history of strong-arming their way into property and flipping it for a bigger profit, but Marty was quick to alleviate those concerns. The bar would remain open under the same name, and only slight alterations would be made to up their profits. Christina and the rest of the staff would stay on. Marty didn't see the need to write that into the contract as he was vocal about the importance of gentleman's agreements in such deals. "Why not just put it into writing?" Michael asked.

"To be honest, kid, that type of language only complicates the sale. You have my word that it'll stay The Whaler with the staff staying on," Marty said with a level of sincerity that ran contrary to the snobbish ways he had previously shown.

As someone who dealt with snake oil salesmen for a living on Wall Street, Michael could smell a fake from a mile away, but Marty strangely seemed like he toed the line between genuine and full of shit in this. Besides, Marty knew real estate in Massachusetts better than almost anyone, and going with him in his area of expertise seemed like a smart business move.

"When can we sign the paperwork?" Michael asked.

"This afternoon. I already have them drawn up, and we can get the pen to paper today, and have the sale signed, sealed, delivered, and reviewed by our lawyers just after Labor Day like you wanted."

"Today?" Michael asked, as he figured he'd need to make at least a few more trips to Boston before anything would be finalized.

"Why not?" Marty said, as he put the documents in front of Michael and put a heavy pen with his name on the side for Michael to actually sign the papers.

Michael stared at the sheets in front of him, and saw the future he imagined being closer than ever with this sudden influx of cash. He briefly fantasized that he traded in Manhattan to settle on the coast, but like Willem Dafoe in *The Last Temptation of Christ*, he dismissed that notion and signed on the dotted line. Once the ink dried, he got up, shook Marty Williams' hand, and headed out to take in the last few days of being a bar owner, a role he never could have imagined himself in just a few short months earlier. He exited the building and ducked into the waiting car outside that would take him back to the Cape for one of the final times as someone with any skin in the bar "game." The ride from Boston to the Cape was shorter than expected on a Friday in the summer, as he managed to get on the road before the real traffic picked up. The weather did him some favors too, since at least a few weekend warriors elected to stay home on account of the miserable conditions. It was still a long enough ride for Michael to ponder not only the long-term future, but the short term as well—how was he going to tell everyone at The Whaler that the bar had been sold and their lives could potentially be turned upside down?

Breaking the news would be rough, but Michael knew he had to do it face to face he owed it to them to tell them that he had signed over their futures. It would come as shock to no one that he had made the sale, as that was pretty much his mission from the day he showed up, but personal relationships and feelings changed the dynamic entirely. Working in an office all day handling countless transactions via phone and email took away from that, and through this sale, he saw that there's a human element that gets lost in the shuffle. He didn't view this side of things as a positive or negative, it was more something that was there that often gets neglected.

On the ride from Boston to Wellfleet, he left Chris Bennett a "Thanks, but no thanks" voicemail six weeks in the making, that unsurprisingly, wasn't returned.

David was working the bar, and happily poured him a new local draft-a far cry from the guy who was ordering martinis with blue cheese olives when he first walked in the door.

"Hey, Mike. Can I ask you something?" Colin said as he approached Michael who was sitting by himself.

"Sure, buddy. You working tonight?" Michael asked, as he realized that despite being "there" for nearly four months, he still had no idea what anyone's schedule was, and at this point, it was too late to really matter.

"No, I'm off," he began. "Can I put my two weeks in with you?"

Michael was perplexed as he technically was the owner, but by the time his two weeks were up, the bar would belong to Marty Williams. "Sure. You get a job somewhere else?"

"Yeah, California, actually. The Dodgers hired me to write for their website and eventually do some prospect work for them," Colin said, without a hint of arrogance, which for a kid who was about to chase a dream 3,000 miles away surely came from the shock of everything changing so quickly.

"That's great news, pal. Let me buy you a beer," Michael said, as he was more than happy for the kid.

"Thanks, boss. I'm still really in shock-it hasn't really set in yet. Anything big happen for you lately?" Colin asked, as his trademark subtle sarcasm returned and a draft beer was put in front of him.

Michael shook his head with a smile and had a laugh. "Yep. I sold the bar. You're the first person to know."

"I thought you liked it down here," Colin said as he was perplexed by what he assumed was a sudden change of heart.

"I do like it around here. I just like Manhattan a bit more, and that's where I work and make money, so it kind of won out."

"Well, congrats."

"Thanks. Here's to new beginnings," Michael said as he raised a glass and toasted his soon-to-be-former barback as they both had plenty of reason to celebrate.

The drink hadn't hit Michael's lips yet when he spied Christina walking in the door. He raced over to intercept her, so he could break the news. She saw him making his way across the room with a somewhat weird sense of urgency and paused.

"Should I be sitting down?" she asked as she pulled a chair from a vacant table before Michael had a chance to answer the question.

"I've got some news," Michael said as he also pulled up a seat from the now chair-less two top.

Christina clearly had an idea of what it was, but chose to deflect reality with a sense of humor.

"You had so much fun in P-Town a few weeks ago that you're batting for the other team now?"

"No, although that would fall under the category of pretty big news," he began with a bit of a chuckle. Then he stopped smiling and took a deep breath. "I sold the bar. The new ownership will be effective the Tuesday after Labor Day."

"Am I out of a job?"

"No," Michael said, reassuringly. "The new owner's keeping it open and keeping you on in your current position."

"Who's the new owner? It's obviously not Brendan, since that would've leaked by now. Word travels quickly down here."

"Martin Williams, Boston real estate guy," he replied, as if he had just sold the bar to Bill Gates and every employee was getting a percentage of his net worth.

"That fucking dickhead?" Christina replied in a tone that got the attention or more than a few patrons and employees of the somewhat quiet bar.

"I take it you don't like him?" Michael asked, confused. In a matter of moments, he went from thinking he made the deal of the century to thinking, "What the fuck have I done?"

"That asshole's bought more bars between Boston and the Vineyard than I care to count, sapped them for money and then turned them into his latest condominiums," Christina said as her shock turned almost to fear. "When I saw his name on the list of potential buyers, I was hoping it was a mistake."

Michael was taken aback with how reaching Marty's reputation was, but felt he had to reassure Christina that it was going to be okay. "Well, actually, he's keeping this spot open. So you've got nothing to worry about."

"Did you get that in writing?"

"I didn't have to, he gave me his word."

"Well, actually," Christina began, with a high level of sass, "I'm no lawyer, but someone's word doesn't hold up in court, so I kind of have every reason to worry about my job and livelihood."

"Just give him a chance-I think this time's gonna be different," Michael said as he realized there was a better than zero percent chance Christina would turn out to be right, but with the ink dried, there wasn't a damn thing he could do.

"Alright, I'll go in with an open mind, but when you're around long enough, you realize these people don't change their ways out of the blue. Maybe I'm wrong, though-you're the expert on making deals."

"Thanks."

"Have you told anyone else yet-namely, Aubrey and Brendan?"

"So far, just you and Colin, who I told kind of off the cuff. I'll break the news to everyone individually this weekend, probably by tonight."

Before he finished his sentence, Aubrey walked in for her shift, and he let her take the time to put her makeup on in the ladies' room and get herself ready. The two had a kiss before she got behind the bar, which Aubrey was quick to point out didn't qualify as a "bar kiss."

"I did something big today." He began, as she clocked in at the computer in front of her.

"You stepped out on me with a heavy-set woman?" she replied as she took his statement and really twisted his words.

"No, Kirstie Alley's out of town for the summer," he began, showing that he still his zingers were the verbal equivalent of a Nolan Ryan fastball. "I sold the bar."

"Really?! I thought this place was growing on you enough that you might keep it!"

"It was the plan all along, and I'm sticking to it."

"Good for you. I'm happy for you," she casually said as she got behind the bar and prepared for a night of slinging beers and keeping the tourists intoxicated. Inside she was shaken up, but she didn't want Michael or anyone else to see her break.

"I've got some news for you too," she continued. "You're not the only one leaving here for the Big City at the end of the summer."

"New York?" Michael said, hoping she was springing on him that she'd be joining him in the Big Apple. For a split second, he imagined their life in New York together-dining at the finest restaurants, going to Broadway plays, catching Rangers games in the nice seats and initiating her into city living.

Aubrey knew her answer would disappoint him, but she laid it out as clearly as possible.

"No. Boston. Got a job lined up with a friend-of-a-friend's real estate company. Market's hot and, as someone once said, the money's in the city."

"That person is regular philosopher-a modern day Aristotle, even," Michael replied. It took him no time to realize that he was the someone she was quoting.

"Why not New York?"

"Way too busy for me," Aubrey began. "I want city living, but not at the speed of the Big Apple, and I want to be close enough to go home and see my parents when I want to."

Michael was at a loss for words as he realized that life was about to come crashing down on both of them. He knew their teenaged-esque summertime love wouldn't last past Labor Day, but the realization that it was coming to an end weighed heavily on him. "Oh," he began, "that makes sense."

"I'm glad it makes sense to you—that's why I'm doing it," Aubrey replied sarcastically before getting to work and leaving Michael drinking his beer by himself.

Not 20 minutes after he informed Aubrey of the sale, he spied Brendan coming in, dirty work clothes and all, for a few beers and a bite to eat. He knew Brendan was a big boy and could handle the rejection, but it wasn't going to be easy, as evidenced by how excited he was to share his plans of purchasing the place a few weeks earlier.

"Brendan, can I talk to you for a quick sec?" Michael said, as he walked across the somewhat empty bar.

"Absolutely. Does it have anything to do with the sale?" he replied, knowing there'd be almost no reason for Michael to talk to him otherwise.

"It does," Michel said with a sigh, as tried to figure out the best way to word the 'thanks, but no thanks' that was about to come.

Before he could do that Brendan beat him to the punch. "Let me guess—you're selling it to somebody else."

"Yeah, I actually already sold it. It'll be someone else's bar a week from Tuesday. Sorry it couldn't work out the way you wanted it to."

"It's fine. I would've loved to have owned this place, but there's more to life than owning a bar. If you don't mind me asking, who actually bought the bar?"

"Martin Williams, a real estate guy from up in Boston."

"Oh, him? I've done some work for him over the years-he owns property everywhere, and always pays on time."

"Did you like him?"

"Seemed nice enough, and his checks never bounced. I was never in business with him, so I don't know that aspect of him, but from my interactions with him, I liked him."

"Good to know," Michael said as he walked away knowing that there was a very good chance that Christina's suspicions about the sale would be all for naught and he wasn't the monster she or anyone else made him out to be. Peace of mind is important and Michael suddenly had plenty of that as he prepared for what would be his penultimate weekend as the owner of The Whaler, and a summer he'd never forget.

For Michael the rest of the weekend played out with a black cloud hanging over him and Aubrey. They had fun together, and were as into one another as ever, but it just felt different. Once again, he knew that what he and Aubrey had almost assuredly wasn't going to carry into the fall, and he was well aware that selling the bar-as expected as it was-would change things for him with the people around The Whaler, but this was a tough pill to swallow. Having the subconscious thought that a good-to-great situation would come to a less-than-storybook ending was a whole different level of pain.

When Sunday morning rolled around, the two were entwined in bed, but Michael needed to hit the road. He'd return for Labor Day weekend, but he had work to do in New York, and this weekend was the unofficial ending of his time on Cape Cod. Labor Day weekend would simply be a money maker for all parties as while Michael would reap the rewards, the ending of the weekend would mean a lot of changes for a lot of people. The clock was ticking, and his car to the airport was less than five minutes away when he got out of bed and hastily got his things together. Within a matter of just over a week, this place would no longer belong to him and he didn't want to leave anything behind.

"I'll see you next weekend. Good ole LBW," Michael said as he gave Aubrey one last kiss before heading for the door.

"Actually, no, you won't," Aubrey began, as she sat up in the bed. "My lease at my place in Boston starts September 1, so I'm moving in Tuesday and Wednesday this week, ahead of Labor Day."

Michael's summer fling, which he thought had developed into something more, screeched to a halt as Aubrey spoke. "Really? Why didn't you tell me that this was it?"

She took a deep breath as a tears began to form in her eyes. "I didn't want it to hurt. I figured shooting you once in the head was better than twice in the leg."

He closed his eyes as he heard the car pull up outside, but his car, flight, and New York in general, couldn't have been more off his radar. He'd just been blindsided like a Lawrence Taylor sack.

"Seriously? We're down to shooting metaphors to describe what we've had and how it's ending?" he said with tears starting to drip down his face.

"Look, I start next week. I'm jumping in with both feet and not looking back. It's all about the future and the future for me is actually putting my degree to use. I'm sorry you're hurt, but I need to do what's best for me," Aubrey said, not 100 percent sure of her plan, as more tears began to run down her face.

"Have fun in Boston," Michael said with that dangerous mix of sadness and anger, as he slammed the door behind him and hopped in the car. Aubrey tried to chase him out the door, but he had already closed the door to the car.

"Floor it the fuck out of here," he implored the driver, as he knew any further conversation would just be adding insult to an already painful emotional injury.

"Is everything okay, sir?" his driver said, with genuine concern, as he looked at his passenger through the rearview mirror.

"I'm fine," Michael declared as he fought through the tears, which were coming at him even harder than they were mere moments earlier.

"Okay, but if you want to talk about it, I'm right here," the driver said once again, with genuine concern for the man in the back seat.

"Thanks, but I'd rather just drown these sorrows in a bottle of bourbon when I get back to New York," he replied, knowing that was exactly what he'd be doing as soon as he was back home.

"Funny thing with that shit is it only masks the pain-it doesn't actually cure anything. Believe me, I've been there before."

"Look, you seem like a nice enough guy, but I don't want to be lectured right now, so-no offense-but can you just drive?" Michael said, knowing how rude it sounded, but he was paying for this ride, and he didn't want a side of a therapy with his airport livery.

The driver just nodded and kept driving. It was an awkward silence for the duration of the ride, but it did end when the pulled up to the airport. From there, Michael just went through the motions as he checked in for his flight and sat quietly in the terminal, reading a free local newspaper. Aubrey had sent him a few texts, but he was ignoring his phone all together-reading a preview of the local high school football teams was a more productive than having a back and forth via text. When it was time to board, all he did was take his seat and stare at the seat in front of him for the duration of the flight. He didn't know how to feel. Sure, the ending was anything but unexpected, and given that he had buried two parents, he knew real grief, but this just sucked. If there was a word to describe feeling nothing, but everything at the same, time that's how Michael felt as the descent into New York began.

15

August 28-29

He took a cab back to Manhattan, and basically threw his stuff into his apartment and headed down to a new local bar. The Tap was two blocks away and between work and travel all summer, he hadn't yet checked it out. Now was the time, as he needed to drown his sorrows like never before. The bar was about a quarter full, as it was a summer Sunday night, which was perfect for Michael, since he didn't want to be bothered.

"Whatever bourbon has the highest alcohol content, with ginger ale. Please," he said to the 20-something hipster-looking bartender in front of him.

"You really want to cut good bourbon with ginger ale?" bartender replied as he clearly was too smart for his own good.

"Yea, I'm paying for it; that's how I want it," Michael fired back, as he was now bordering on completely angry. Who was this young punk to tell him how to drink his booze?

"I'm just saying as a bartender."

"Let me cut you off right there. I own a fucking bar, so don't tell me how to do this," Michael said as he was now completely seething.

"You got it," the bartender said as he realized it was in his best interest to just shut up and let the customer have what he wanted.

"Thanks," Michael said as he took a swig from the rocks glass and got what he had been coveting since he got out of bed.

"Are you a bourbon guy?" the bartender asked, trying to lighten the pretty tense air that had developed around the two of them.

"Nope, I fucking hate it. Needed something to take the edge off a day that can best be described as a living fucking hell," Michael said nonchalantly, as he took a second massive sip and finished the contents of the glass. "Keep it coming, though."

"Yes sir," the bartender said with a look of shock on his face as even with the mixer that was a healthy amount of alcohol put down almost effortlessly. When he came back with another drink the bartender had a wily smile on his face.

"This one's on me. Least I can do for being such a know-it- all earlier. My name's Barry, by the way," he said, as he reached out his hand.

"Nice to meet you, Barry. Michael O'Reilly. At least you're aware of being a know-it-all,—some assholes spend their life legislating the details of other people's lives. Water under the bridge, buddy," Michael said as he took a slightly smaller, more civilized sip.

"Bourbon under the bridge," Barry said with a smile and walked away to tend to another guest.

Two drinks turned to three and three turned to five and the next thing Michael knew, it was almost 1 am, and he had to be up for work in a matter of hours. "Fuck," he said loud enough for the other patrons to hear. "Barry, can I close out?"

"Sure," he replied as he gave him his tab.

"$150 for seven drinks. I forgot where I am," Michael said, examining the bill and coming to grips with the fact that it costs money to drink at places other than The Whaler, and, in New York, it costs a lot of money.

"That top shelf stuff isn't cheap," Barry replied, as he was in "don't shoot the messenger" mode.

"Nothing worth having is," Michael fired back, as he thought about how much of a shitshow the previous day had been. "Here, take this for your troubles."

He put five $100 bills on the bar.

"Dude, are serious? Thank you!" Barry said as he tried to imagine how big his tip would've been had he not been a dick earlier.

"Don't mention it. I'm fucking rich and I'm gonna be richer next week," Michael said, slurring each word more than the last.

"I guess I'll have to check out the bar you own someday," Barry said.

"Don't. It sucks and it won't be mine after next week. The money will be, and the money can buy me fun times like this," he finished, as he walked out the door and began the crawl back to his apartment.

When he got inside, he laid on his couch and contemplated the absolute mess he put himself in. He had to be at his desk in six hours and he was nowhere near the top of his game. He was still wired and decided it was worth giving Aubrey a call-because calls and conversations like that are best with copious amounts of alcohol involved. As expected, she didn't answer as even for someone that worked in an industry centered around weird hours, it was late and she was assuredly asleep. That didn't stop Michael, as voicemail is a thing for a reason, so he let it rip.

"Baby, it's me," he began, in a drunken stupor. "It's early, I don't why you're not up, but anyway I love you and want you to come to New York. We can live here and do fun shit and you can shop and we can go to Central Park. So much fun stuff. Boston sucks-lousy city; don't move there, you're too classy for that. I love you; call me in the morning so we can make it happen."

Within minutes of putting his phone down Michael was passed out on the couch and in a slumber that would make a hibernating grizzly bear proud. He hadn't set an alarm, but luckily for him the construction work outside chose to start earlier than it was supposed to. Waking up to the sounds of a jack hammer, in addition the countless other indistinguishable sounds of the city, he was in a bit of a panic. He wasn't in a race against time, but his head was in agony. He felt like he would hurl up everything he had ever eaten, and he had a few missed calls and a text from Aubrey. In her text, she told him that she loved him too, but the timing wasn't great, but had he chosen to stay in Wellfleet-which was something he never seriously considered-maybe she would have altered her plans, and that if he was ever in Boston, to give her a call. It was a slight change of tone from 24 hours earlier, but it made sense to him, once the initial shock wore off, cooler heads tend to prevail.

He thought about calling her back, but he didn't have the time or energy to have a full-on discussion with Aubrey. It was a moot point anyway, as she'd be moving into her new apartment in a day, and within a week, The Whaler would-officially-no longer be his. Down the line, would she be worth reaching out to? Absolutely, but there were bigger fish to fry for him at this very moment.

"Off to work," he thought aloud as he forced himself into the coldest shower allowed by New York law, hoping the frigid water would douse the fire in his head. The shower did him almost no good, nor did the gallon of tap water, fresh from the Hudson River, alleviate the pain. He would have to wheel and deal on the floor with a hangover that should have been tested for steroids before being allowed to enter his body. Like everyone, Michael had worked hung over more times than he cared to count, but working the morning after having a good time is a far cry from working the morning after attempting to drown every negative feeling in alcohol. With designer sunglasses on his face, he headed out the door and into a sultry New York morning that only made his symptoms worse. The air conditioning in his building came to his body like manna from heaven, and while it was going to hurt like a mother fucker, the ideal indoor conditions today were going to be survivable. At 10 am, he was called into a meeting about a big sale that could make the firm and him a lot of money. He was tempted to come up with some bullshit reason he couldn't make it, since he was going to make a lot of money on his own shortly, but this is was the kind of thing he came to Wall Street for in the first place.

Begrudgingly, he sat at the big table and prepared for Charlie's speech on how this was a deal worth pursuing and that the team should do everything in their power to get it done. Sure as the day is long, that was exactly the spiel him and a select few other brokers were getting from Charlie-this time, a deal to buy a Midwest trucking conglomerate that had fallen on hard times. Interesting stuff for sure, Michael assumed, but his brain was anywhere but in that boardroom and he was zoned out for the entire hour he sat there. When the meeting was adjourned, Charlie cornered Michael on his way out the door.

"Everything alright, Michael?" he asked. "You seemed off in there."

"Yeah, I'll be fine," Michael said, knowing he had been caught red-handed mailing it in for a pretty important meaning.

"Rough weekend at the beach?" Charlie asked, trying to get a grip on this unusual behavior from an otherwise professional's professional.

"No, too much to drink when I got in last night. Won't happen again."

"You're alright, you're young. Take in the perks of living in the City while you can, because before you know it, you'll be older and living in suburbia."

"Don't want that," Michael replied, as it had been a minute since he lived in Jersey, and he was in no rush to go back anytime soon.

"How *is* the bar up there?" Charlie asked.

"I sold it, effective next week. Hopefully the check clears by the end of the month," Michael said, thinking of the massive chunk of change that was going to enter his bank account.

"Good man, made your money up there all summer, surely fucked a barmaid or two, and now you're cashing out. You're good, kid." Charlie gleefully said, not knowing the barmaid reference struck a bit of a nerve with Michael.

"Yup, I played it exactly how I wanted it," Michael said with a hint of defeat He did make money all summer, and then flipped the bar for a huge profit, but his heart took a bit of a hit in the process.

"Good. Glad this is over, with no more short weeks and long weekends spent in Massachusetts for one of my best brokers."

"Thank you for letting me do that this summer-it really made things easier for me," Michael said with gratitude, but also with the understanding that he wasn't getting away with leaving a day early for his Labor Day weekend trip-his last as owner of The Whaler.

"Don't mention it—just make sure you have the fastball when we follow up on this in a few weeks. This could be huge for all of us," Charlie said, as he walked down the hall and out of sight.

"Yes, sir," Michael fired back as he turned to go back to his desk as his head hurt only slightly less than it had when he woke up. "This week is gonna suck"

To his own shock, Michael survived that Monday from hell, and found himself laying in front of his air conditioner watching lousy movies on the couch by 7:30 pm. As he laid there, his mind wandered to the big deals that were at hand, and how much he'd need to be at the top of his game in the next few weeks. He also thought about his travel plans for the weekend as Charlie-who had been lenient all summer-without saying as much, told him he wasn't ducking out of work early on Friday, so his whole weekend was backed up. Flying in Saturday morning and heading back to New York on Monday afternoon seemed to be the smartest play. All of the paperwork for the sale had been taken care of, so all he had to do when he was up there was make sure his keys and a few other things were left behind for when the new ownership took over. Christina had set aside some of Danny's personal effects that she thought Michael would like, but he really didn't care for any of it. The only thing he ever got from his uncle that mattered was that bar, and he was about to profit mightily off it. He also planned on leaving the furniture in his uncle's old apartment, as it was somewhat new, and the Williamses could surely find better use for it then he could. It was going to be an emotional weekend, but it had to be done, and he was going to ensure it was done correctly.

16

September 5

There is no depression like that of Labor Day weekend, especially Labor Day itself, and especially in a place like New England, where it signals the end of three months of beauty and the start of the countdown to winter. For Michael, it was almost on steroids as he turned over the last of his keys and paperwork to the Williams family and prepared to leave Wellfleet and head back to Manhattan. The weekend was the personification of morose, and while his bank account would benefit, it still felt weird to just up and leave. He arrived in town on Saturday morning and over the next 48 hours, took in what he was giving up and reminded himself that it would all be worth it, because it would help him get where he wanted to be-in the upper part of the Manhattan totem pole. But saying goodbye to people he had come to know wasn't as easy as he originally thought it would be.

It was unseasonably cold and dreary on that Monday-the scene looked more like something from the Midwest in October than New England at the end of summer-as he prepared to leave The Whaler one final time. With the exception of Brendan, who had stopped by for his early afternoon Budweiser, and Christina, who pretty much lived in the bar, almost none of his summertime acquaintances were there to see him off. Obviously, Aubrey was up in Boston; Colin had just gotten to La-La Land, and according to his texts, was set up and excited about being around a major league team; and Dave was not the type to be up on a Monday to see off a now-former boss. Likewise, most of the regulars from the summer had either left the Cape for the season, or in the case of the locals, had spent the weekend anywhere but on Cape Cod. He entered the summer looking to sell the place for a profit, and that he did, but a weird sort of bond had formed between him and this little stretch of land on Cape Cod Bay.

"Damn shame we couldn't work something out," Brendan said; while he did have a bit of an axe to grind over finishing second, he didn't let it show in his interactions with Michael.

"It happens, man-you're a good guy. Glad to have spent some time with you trying to get something done," Michael said, though, at the end of the day, he got the deal that *he* wanted.

"We'll miss ya; come back and visit," Christina said, though she knew there was a better chance of seeing JFK's ghost walk into the bar than of seeing him before the summertime, as nothing about him screamed offseason Cape Cod type.

"I might come by next summer." he answered, though he himself wasn't sure how truthful that statement was.

"I look forward to it," Christina said knowing that if she *was* still around in a year that meant that Marty had kept his word and she still had a job.

As their conversation wound down, Michael's black car was pulling up, and it was finally time to leave.

"Good luck, buddy," Christina said as he got into the car.

"You, too," Michael said. Then his car pulled away and went down the road, south, towards Hyannis.

As soon as the car got out of sight, Brendan raised a question that had been on his mind all weekend. "So, who the hell is in charge now?"

"Me, I guess," Christina said, as she herself wasn't sure the answer to that question. "The Williams' guy is coming by tomorrow, so I guess it'll be business as usual after that. Until then, it'll be like the few months between Danny dying and Michael showing up."

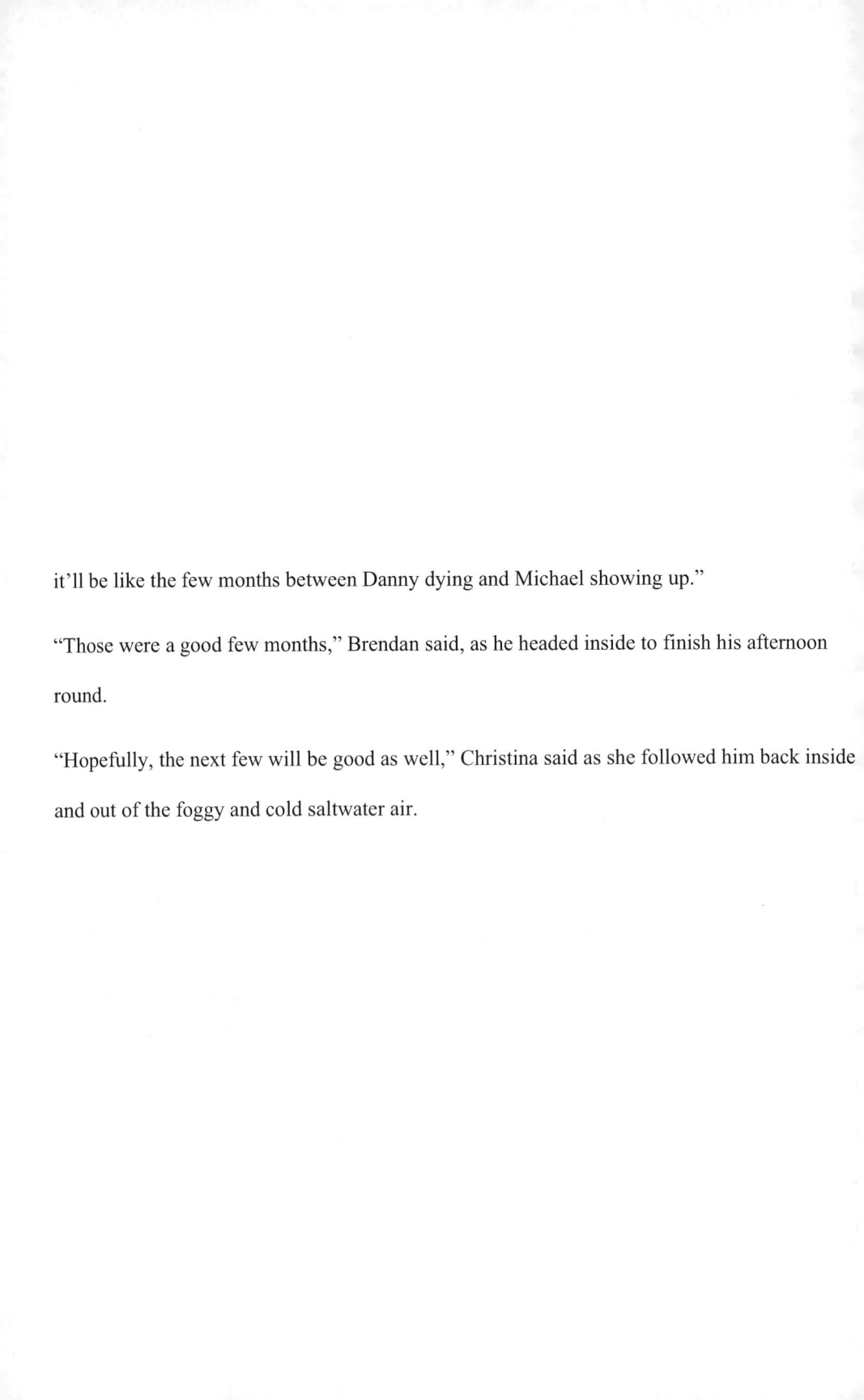

"Those were a good few months," Brendan said, as he headed inside to finish his afternoon round.

"Hopefully, the next few will be good as well," Christina said as she followed him back inside and out of the foggy and cold saltwater air.

__17__

October 3

It was an afternoon in early October when Michael stepped out of the office for a minute and saw a missed call and a voicemail from a Massachusetts number. The message was short and anything but sweet as Christina's voice teetered on the edge of all out panic.

"The bar's getting torn down and seasonal cottages are going in. Williams played you, and fucked all of us, royally."

Michael put his phone away and just stared off into 3rd Avenue the way you would if you found out your entire family was killed by a pack of wolves. There were no tears, no expletive-laced tirades, just shock mixed with confusion, sadness, and anger all rolled into one. How could someone who spent his entire life in business allow himself to be hustled and allow this situation? Only one word could come to mind to describe just how bad the situation was.

"Fuck," Michael said, as he slowly lifted his arm to hail a cab back to his apartment.

From the moment he met Marty, there had been a stench of snake oil salesman to him, but even Michael hadn't seen this one coming. Working on Wall Street and being kept within the confines of the office for what seemed like 24/7 took the human element out of doing business. Deals were made with the bottom line intact, and if that meant "lower level" people lost their jobs as a result, it didn't matter, so long as you increased your net worth. The time he spent in Wellfleet, changed his view of this, as he spent time with-and got to put a human face to-the people who would soon be out of work and hurting while his bank account grew. Likewise, Marty seemed like someone who legitimately gave a shit about the year-rounders on Cape Cod—and wouldn't pull a stunt at their expense in exchange for a few more dollars in his already deep pockets. Michael quickly phoned Marty Williams to figure out why he'd violate the gentleman's agreement they had to keep the bar operating and the employees working. When Marty finally picked up his ringing phone, all Michael could muster up was "How could you do this?"

"Nothing was signed-I was well within my rights to change my mind when a better opportunity presented itself. Hell, as a big time broker on Wall Street, you of all people should know that the bottom line comes first," Martin said in his old money tone that just reeked of Boston College snobbery that everyone Massachusetts native from Beverley to Bridgewater can tell you about.

"Bullshit! You were never going to keep the Whaler open-you just threw out a smokescreen to blind me and move right in," Michael replied, wondering to himself how he could be such a damn moron to let someone like this play him like a fiddle.

"That may be the case, but you can't be mad at me for making a shrewd business decision. I bought the bar and the liquor license for $3 million and when I'm done tearing it down and building two cottages, I'll be able to rent them for two grand a week each during the summer. My investment will pay for itself within a few years, and then I'll be able to flip each of them for a profit. With the bullshit blue laws in this state, a liquor license is worth an easy six figures *by itself.*"

"I want a Billy Martin, Michael said, referencing the endless second chances George Steinbrenner gave the former Yankee skipper. "Let me buy it back from you for what you paid, plus some extra party favors."

"This isn't the back nine at Pebble Beach," Martin said. "There aren't any mulligans in this line of work, kid." He made their argument over real estate sound like a daytime segment on ESPN 4.

"*If* I were to sell it back to you, I'd want the original price *plus* $750,000 and *if* this were to happen, I'd want the paper drawn up by the end of the week."

"Let me think about it," Michael said as realizing he was about to bite off way more than he could chew, no matter how this deal went down.

"The clock is ticking, kid," Martin said, and hung up the phone.

All Michael could think about were the people who depended on that little shithole bar a stone's throw from the Atlantic. He gave them his word-and their lives were about to be ruined because he had been looking out for his own bank account.

"Well," he said as he gazed into his bedroom wall. "This is a tough son of a bitch."

While he really hadn't spent any of the money he got in the sale-he extent of his lavish spending so far was some new suits, a $500 Rolex, and a few bar tabs, of course-Michael knew he was going to be getting a hefty income tax bill from Uncle Sam come the end of the year. If he were to try to buy the bar back, he'd need to start borrowing, and his dream of *owning* in Manhattan would go up in smoke faster than a Southern California wildfire. Without even adding the additional $750,000, this wouldn't be as simple as transferring the money from his account into Marty Williams'. As he sat at his kitchen table and weighed the options, the only certainty was the Williams family could not end up with the Whaler, and if it meant cannibalizing all he had worked for to make his dreams come true in Manhattan, then so be it. In his eyes, buying The Whaler and keeping it open was his way of atoning for the ignorance he had displayed over his years on Wall Street and the hurt his greed probably caused countless people. If that meant walking away from Wall Street and down the line a potential seven-figure-per-year paycheck to run a bar on a stretch of beach in Massachusetts then so be it.

It also dawned on Michael that he and his late Uncle weren't that different in that they let their respective dreams hurt those around him. The more Michael thought about it, the more it made sense that Danny's never-ending misery and uncanny ability to push people away stemmed from his failed hockey career. Being cut because he was born in New Jersey and not New Brunswick formed the foundation of what would be a life of alienating everyone and making life impossible for those unlucky enough to have to work for him. Likewise, Michael got caught up in the game and adding to his net worth and completely disregarded the good people upon whose backs he had been making his fortune. How many deals had he been involved with that had a terrible impact on people he'd never see? Even as a broker, someone not directly involved in what happened before and after such deals he knew the Williams debacle wasn't the first time his quest for money had hurt others, but it would be the last.

With all these thoughts racing through his head, it was tough to fall asleep, but he knew he had a long week ahead of him, and getting even a couple hours was a hell of a lot better than staying up all night. When his alarm went off at 6:45, he was uncharacteristically sluggish not even three cups of strongly brewed joe could get him ready to tackle *this* day. As he gazed out his window at Manhattan's craziness, he muttered, "Today's going to be a shitshow from hell."

No sooner did he get the vulgarity out of his mouth, then his phone started having a seizure on his bed. The first text he saw was from Aubrey and it was a simple enough "How could you let this happen?"; clearly, she heard the news and wasn't happy about it. Before he could reply, he had a received a much longer message from Aubrey- that went into detail about how much of a low-life he was and to never bother calling, texting or emailing her ever again because as of now he was blocked on all mediums. His pain and regret he felt was now amplified by the closest thing he had to the love of his life telling him just how badly he had fucked up and just how hypocritical he was. Getting through this day on the floor would be one of the biggest challenges he had ever undertaken. He wasn't his usual bright eyed and bushy tailed self when he left his apartment that morning.

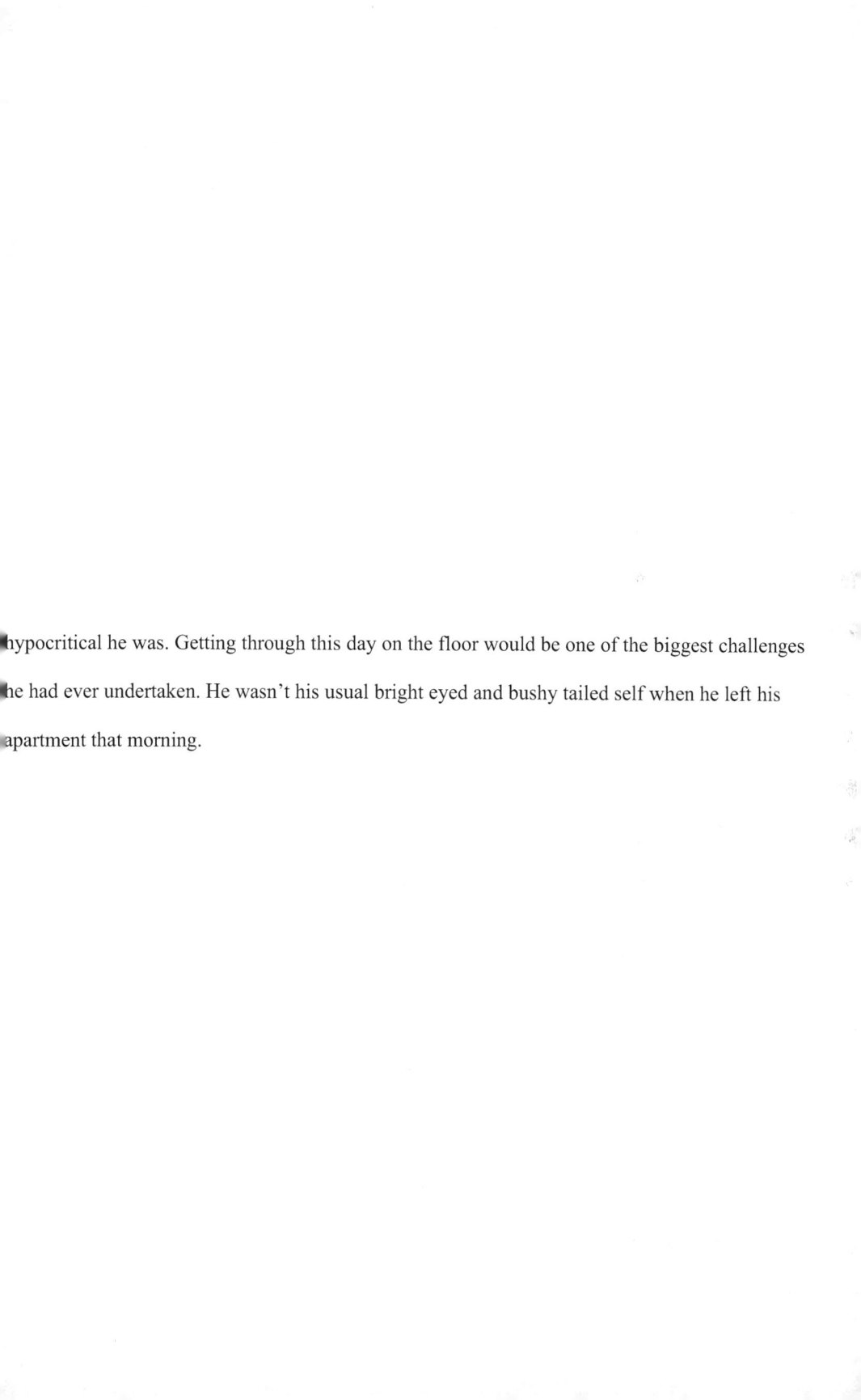

18

October 4-5

When he did get to his office, he was called into a meeting regarding the sale of the trucking company that would make Michael and his colleagues a healthy commission. The plan was to buy controlling interest in the company, sell off a certain number of shares and then outsource the work to a plant in Windsor, Ontario that would do the same runs through the Midwest and Southern Ontario for significantly cheaper given the exchange rate. While the conditions were being explained to Michael and his colleagues, all he could do was stare off into space and think long and hard about the drivers, mechanics, and loaders who would be out of work and the looks of shame they'd have as they told their families that they had failed them and were no longer employed. People on that end of the spectrum don't get brought up on Wall Street, even though it's their suffering that allows brokers like Michael to further pad their wealth. While the final terms were being discussed, Michael simply couldn't take it for another second.

"Have any of you guys put any thought into the people who are gonna get fucked royally in this deal?"

"I beg your pardon?" Charlie Ortoli said to him, as he couldn't quite believe what had just come out his protégé's mouth.

"Seriously. We're all going to make a boatload of money on this deal, then celebrate with bar tabs that are bigger than the monthly mortgage payments that these people won't be able to pay anymore," Michael said, as he looked around at the room full of his soon-to-be his former friends and colleagues.

"When the fuck did you become Charlie Sheen in that goddamned movie? Did being around shanty dwellers in Massachusetts get you thinking like a poor person and less like the hot shot broker you've proven yourself to be?"

"Fuck you, Charlie. All I wanted to be growing up was a broker, but looking at you and the crooked shit you pull 24/7, and the fact you'd rather chase around cocktail waitresses than go home to your wife and kids is like seeing a poster on what not to aspire to be," Michael said, knowing he had already dug his own grave. He might as well go out with a few parting shots at the old geezer, he thought as he began to get up and make his grand exit.

"You'll never work in this town again, O'Reilly. I'll make sure of that, you ungrateful little fuck," Charlie said as Michael made his final approach for the door.

"I wouldn't work here for all the money on the Upper East Side," Michael called back as he closed the door literally and metaphorically on his days as a broker. Cleaning out his office took almost no time, which was fine, because by the time he had the essentials packed up, a security guard was ready to escort him out the door like he was some sort of criminal.

The stories behind each of the people in the sea of humanity on the streets of Manhattan are as unique as the people they belong to. So the image of Michael O'Reilly, top buttons unbuttoned and tie anywhere but around his neck, carrying the moving box with office trinkets and surfing the waves of people was a picture worth a couple thousand words. In the span of a few hours, he had burned every bridge he'd worked so hard to build and through it all, he couldn't help but smile. On the outside, he looked like another dejected guy who took a bite out of the Big Apple and got the maggots, but on the inside he felt a simple and beautiful type of happiness that only comes through what others may perceive as failure. Sometimes the ugliest moments bring us the most beautiful feelings and going through a shitstorm brings us to an anything but shitty results.

When he did get back to his apartment, Michael laid out all the paperwork and began crunching some numbers. His antics that led to his departure from Wall Street-and his very well-paying job-would mean any hope of buying the bar and continuing to live in New York went out the window. Likewise, he knew that in order for the place to truly run at its highest levels of efficiency, he'd need to be there. This truly was all or nothing, and if he was going to make this purchase, he better damn well look at every possible angle. He figured that with some help in the form of loans and a co-financier, the deal that Marty Williams offered him was doable. As he poured himself a glass of Jack Daniels and stared at the countless sheets of paper spread over his kitchen table, he made his decision.

"Fuck it, let's do this," he whispered to himself as he pressed the glass to his lips. Usually when he closed big deals, he popped drastically overpriced bottles of champagne, but this time was different and his beverage of choice was a nice reflection of his new destiny-tough, at times hard to swallow, but 100 percent American.

Despite no longer having a job, Michael was still up at the crack of dawn, and like most days on the floor, he was on the phone for most of it, trying to close a big deal. The irony was the money he was trying to piece together to buy back the bar was peanuts compared to what he usually dealt with, but unlike most of his deals, this was real money that he needed ASAP—and a lot of it was his. When it was all said and done, he was able to, through his own money and a generous loan from a former Columbia classmate working at Wells Fargo, gather 90 percent of what he needed to make the repurchase. He was still short and desperate, meaning there was only one place to turn, and with that in mind, he placed the make-or-break call.

He took a deep breath as the phone rang twice, before a familiar voice picked up.

"Hello, Brendan, it's Michael O'Reilly. How's it going?" Michael said, as he began what was sure to be a tense conversation.

"Oh. Hi, Michael. Are you taking a break from rat-fucking the little people to talk to me?" Brendan asked as he tried to hold back an even more expletive-laced tirade.

"Yep, once I get off the phone with you, I'm gonna rob a hospice and then tell a bunch of school children that Santa Claus isn't real," Michael said while trembling, hoping a sick, twisted sense of humor would be enough to defuse the tension.

"Just as I expected!" Brendan said with a bit of a chuckle. "To what do I owe the pleasure of your call?"

"I'm buying the bar back-or trying to, anyway-and I need some help to break the plane and get this done," Michael said while breathing a sigh of relief that his twisted humor had worked to a tee.

"I thought you'd never ask," Brendan said. "What were you thinking? Someone to go 50/50 with and banish those douchebag Williamses as far away from Wellfleet as possible?"

"Actually I need the final piece. Would you be in for $250,000 for 10 percent? I'm at the goal line; I just have to punch the damned thing in. I can have the paperwork to you by tomorrow."

"That's the thing-I want a bigger piece of the action. I'll give you $500,000 for a 40 percent stake. Plus, I make the calls regarding the septic system and the countless other things that need repairs in that laborer's nightmare."

Michael was torn; on the one hand, he'd have the funds to get the deal immediately with some more of his own cash to hold on to, but his original figures would be off and he'd have to relinquish a portion of potential control.

"I want as much control as possible. I don't know if I can go to 40 percent."

"Kid, control is a sonnovabitch, and possibly the last thing you should be looking to assert over anyone right now. That's my final offer-take it, or let the asshole Williams family ruin the lives of a lot of great people."

Michael could only stare off into space as he pondered what would be the biggest decision of his business career.

"Deal. But I get to live upstairs, rent free," Michael said with a sigh as he was now 60 percent owner of a bar he was 100 percent owner of a few weeks earlier and a few months earlier, had barely known existed.

"That's fine. So, I get 40 percent, and pay for the new septic system and you live upstairs and hold down that fort?"

"Sounds about right. I'll have the paperwork drawn up, and get this all done by the end of the week," Michael said, as he came to grips with the somewhat unfavorable circumstances surrounding this sale.

Once the phone conversation ended, Michael called Marty Williams, who, to his credit, kept the deal they agreed to, and gave the greenlight for the sale. In a weird way, this may have been Marty's best deal in a long time; as he made a solid profit on an investment by simply holding on to it for a weeks. As ruthless and money-hungry as he was, he was more than happy to take his cash and move on to the next deal.

19

Morning/Afternoon, October 6

While Michael had looked into costs for a potential move to uptown Manhattan, the thought of moving everything he owned to an already furnished place in Wellfleet was more than moronic, as was just leaving everything he had. So, without packing a thing, he used the internet to his advantage, and within an afternoon, the apartment was empty, and he had a few bucks in his pocket as he sold anything that didn't hold practical or sentimental value.

Rather than sit around an empty apartment, Michael decided to head up to the Cape and start his new life early. Unlike previous trips, there'd be no gaudy black car picking him up at the airport to show off his importance; rather, Brendan-now his business partner-would pick him. Less glamorous, but more efficient-and this was the reality of his new way of life.

When it was time to go Michael looked around at the barren walls of his apartment and thought about the past. The counters where he poured enough bottles of wine to flood a city block were empty, and the bedroom where he got lucky with a socialite or two was now just a wide open space-or as wide open as you can get in an 80 square foot room. Rather than waste his time thinking about every memory he'd made there, it was time to go. It was 6 pm, and he had a flight to the Cape, and the start of his new life, at 9. He was packing light this time around, as all of his earthly belongings were all sold or in boxes en route to the Cape so it was just a duffle bag he grabbed as he walked out the door for the final time. He left his key and a thank you for his landlord in his mailbox and went outside to get his cab to LaGuardia

On the way out the door for the final time he saw Sean the doorman, paper in hand, getting ready to listen a preseason Knicks/Nets game with the same passion as if it were Game 7 of the Finals.

"Are you really leaving?" the ever inquisitive former detective asked.

"Yes sir. Trading the urban jungle for the beach and a bar."

Sean had a laugh as he looked up and down at the youngster he had come to really like. "Me, too. Leave for Miami Beach next month-time for the wife and I to enjoy what we've been working for. Fuck this craziness."

"Well, play a round of golf for me when you get there," Michael said as he realized that while they were going in different directions they were seeking the same thing-an escape from the way of life that had chained them down with monotony. Unlike Sean, Michael would have more than a few years of work ahead of him before he could put his feet up and down mai tais, but compared to the way his life was now, it sure as hell would feel like a vacation.

"Kid, I'm from the Bronx. I've never played a round of golf in my life. Hell, if I had a golf club in my house growing up, it would've been to beat burglars to death."

"Then have a drink for me, and we'll call it even."

"Will do, son, and if I ever make it up to Massachusetts, I'll come by and let you buy me a drink."

"You've got yourself a deal, Sean. Boss's honor," Michael said as he reached out his hand to Sean. Sean laughed at the gesture, got up, pushed his chair in and gave Michael a big hug, which was anything but his usual style.

"You're a good kid. Best of luck up there," Sean said as he looked at Michael, eye to eye.

"Yes, sir. I'll try not to tell anyone of your new found means of showing affection," Michael slyly replied.

"Tell anyone I'm giving hugs and I'll drive up there and beat you myself. Word gets out and everyone will want one, and foot traffic will be backed up to the damn Hudson."

Michael gave Sean one final pat on the back and headed outside and got himself a cab. The ride to LaGuardia was the usual mix of frustrating and scenic that driving in New York entails. LaGuardia sits just over the river from Manhattan, and the ride over there was as much a transition as you can find on any eight mile drive in America. The East River may be a far cry from the mighty Mississippi, in terms of serving as a line of division, but it is a New York landmark that is as much a part of the city's geography as anything else, mostly because it separates Manhattan from the Communist Republic of Brooklyn. Michael spent a year living in Brooklyn, and the ride through the borough reminded him of how much his past served as a springboard for where he was going.

When he got out of the cab outside the terminal, Michael took one last gasp of city air before he readied for his flight north. New York's air may have an unhealthy amount of pollution in it, but to Michael, it tasted like home, and it quickly dawned on him that he'd miss little things like this. Otherwise annoying things like the air quality-or lack thereof-and the scientifically unique scent that comes from a subway car, had weird sentimental meanings. He'd miss the many positives of living in the Big Apple, where everything from a steak dinner to a new shirt was within walking distance at any hour of the day. But it was time to move on. He had a flight to catch, and standing in the middle of a terminal thinking about the past wasn't getting him on that plane.

20

Evening, October 6

The flight up the coast offered Michael another glimpse into just how much his life was going to change. From a mile up, he could clearly see the hustle and bustle of New York as dusk descended on the city. That gave way to the massive expanse that is the state of Connecticut. The Nutmeg State gave way to Narragansett Bay on the coast of America's tiniest state, and eventually, he was over Massachusetts. Buzzards Bay turned into Cape Cod Bay, and by the time the final descent began, he was more at peace with his decision than ever before. The frigid burst of fall air Michael was expecting to hit him like a linebacker wasn't there, since the Cape was going through an Indian Summer this week, and even at this late hour the temperature was more than bearable. Walking out of the terminal into that salty air, he spied Brendan's pickup waiting patiently for him.

"Howdy stranger," Brendan said as Michael slid into his passenger door and threw his duffle bag in the back.

"Am I in Texas or Cape Cod right now?" Michael answered as he took in a breath of ocean air before slamming the door shut.

"You're not in Kansas anymore kiddo," Brendan answered as he began speeding towards Wellfleet.

"What's the rush?" Michael asked, as he thought not contracting a livery driver would mean not having to be driven around like Dale Sr. was in the driver's seat, but alas here he was going more than a little over the speed limit on the backroads of the Cape.

"I have a surprise for you, and I think you'll like it," Brendan said, with a bit of a chuckle as he could see Michael may have needed a lot of things, but speed apparently wasn't one of them. "We have to swing by my place to get it, though."

"I can only imagine what it is," he replied as his mind began racing almost as fast as the car as to what Brendan could have in store for him.

The truck pulled up in front of Brendan's house, and they both got and were hit by a sea breeze right away the temperature may have been higher than the norm, but the seabreeze acted as a means of leveling. Brendan then asked Michael the question that had been on his mind the entire ride.

"You have a driver's license, right?"

"Yeah. I haven't used it as anything more than a form of ID in years, but it is valid and current per the good people at the New York State DMV," he replied, not knowing where this conversation was headed.

"And you haven't gotten a car yet, have you?"

"No, why?"

"You'll need one to get around down here, I'm not sure if you know, but there aren't any subway stops around here," Brendan said, as he pointed to a candy apple red Ford truck in his driveway. "All yours, my friend."

"This is your idea of a party favor?" Michael asked, since while he was appreciative.

"Yup, may not be a bottle of bubbly, like you white collar types are used to, but it sure as hell is practical."

"I really just don't know what to say."

"Well around here, when someone gets you a present we usually say 'thank you;' not sure if that's how they do it in the Tri-State area."

Embarrassed by his perceived lack of manners, Michael blurted out "Thank you!" before going over and analyzing his new baby.

"You're welcome. It's not exactly brand new, but it'll comfortably get you from A to B."

"If you don't mind me asking, where'd this come from? You only had the one truck last time I was here."

"It was impounded. A buddy of mine is cop that owed me a favor, so he may or may not have changed some things around in the paperwork so I could commandeer it. I also figured it'd be the perfect welcoming present for you."

"Well, thanks again. I can't wait to hit the road with this."

"Why wait? Drive her to the bar tonight, and get to know the roads a little bit while you're at it. You do know how to get there from here right?"

"I guess my old friend Mr. GPS will have to show the way," Michael laughed.

"Use that for now, but get used to driving around here," Brendan suggested. "I think you'll be here a while."

"That's the plan…it's not like I'll have any job offers lined up on Wall Street anytime soon, and given the amount of money I put into this place, the only way I could afford to live in Manhattan would be if my roommate was a sewer rat,." Michael said as he reflected on what a different world he was now living in.

"We don't have any sewer rats around here-the occasional dune mouse, but nothing bigger that a salt shaker."

"Good. Not for nothing, but what's the deal with insurance and registration and all that shit for this? I honestly haven't had anything to do with having my name on a car in a long time," Michael asked, as he gestured towards the truck.

"It's all registered in my name; we'll transfer it over later. What is it with you big city types and paperwork?"

"If it's not written down, then it doesn't matter, and I may have learned that the hard way, if you didn't know."

"Touché. But just get yourself home tonight and we'll tackle the paperwork beast and administrative shit tomorrow."

"Sounds good. I can't thank you enough,." Michael said as he got into *his* truck and readied for the journey that was only a few miles, but given how late it was, how spotty his GPS service was, and his overall rustiness behind the wheel, the trip took a little longer than expected. He didn't care, though—-riving the ocean view roads of Cape Cod brought him a sense of freedom that being packed like a sardine in New York never did. When he did finally pull up to The Whaler, it was past 1 am and, since it was a week night, the bar had been closed for a few hours. The temperature was starting to dip, and it was almost pitch black out, but here Michael stood in front of what was now his home. A lot of his stuff had been delivered, and more would be coming in the days to follow, but it felt homely enough, and when he put his head to the pillow he fell asleep with a clearer conscience than even he could have imagined.

21

October 7

Much like he did when he was working as a broker, he was still up at the crack of dawn. It was the first day of the rest of his life, and he needed to be ready to tackle whatever came his way. By 8 am, he'd made the mini office downstairs that once belonged to Danny all his-he was the boss in this place now. Was it a tenth story corner office with a killer view? No, it was in the basement of a place a stone's throw from the ocean that had a few leaks, but it was *his* and that's all that mattered. At about 10 am, Christina walked in, shocked to see him so comfortable so soon.

"I didn't think we'd see you here for a while," she declared.

"Well, I figured I might as well come right in and get to work. I want that septic system taken care of before the winter makes it borderline impossible. That and I want to see what we can do to increase sales during what's otherwise a slow time of year."

"Okay then, let's get to work," Christina said as she put her coffee down and prepared to go over a few ideas that Michael had written down on the pad of paper in front of him. "Good to have you back, by the way."

"Good to be back," he replied, without the slightest bit of crass attitude that had come to define him around The Whaler.

"So, what brought the change of heart?" Christina said as Michael settled into his new office.

"I beg your pardon?"

"What was it that made you go from ruthless broker in the concrete jungle, to essentially being a run of the mill bar owner in the middle of nowhere that happens to have a beach?"

"Humanity. That's what did it. What good is it to make a shit load of money if you have to break the backs of the people that got you there? Sure, the big city is a more glamorous way of life on the outside, but you're dead inside and that's not a healthy way to go through life," Michael said, sounding more like a philosopher than a businessman for the first time in his life.

"Well, thanks. Doubt that'll be enough to win back Aubrey, though," Christina said as she knew what Michael really wanted more than making things right and owning a bar was getting Aubrey's heart back.

Michael just looked at Christina with a thousand yard stare and asked the question that had been burning inside him since Aubrey's last fateful text message.

"Have you spoke to her at all since she left?"

"Yeah, just before I knew you were buying it back. She's livid at you-it'll take a lot more than a call or a text," Christina said, even though she knew that wasn't what Michael wanted to hear.

22

Afternoon, October 10

Aubrey had continued ignoring his calls and texts, but Michael knew he had to get through to her, no matter what. Luckily for Michael, he ran a Google search and that indicated she had just started as real estate broker in South Boston. Michael headed to the Hub and found her office on the neighborhood's main drag. As he walked through the door, he had a flashback to visiting his mother at work back in the day and how much he resented her old office. If Wall Street people were stuck up, at least they had a reason-they were mostly all rich-but real estate agents in suburban Jersey in Michael's eyes were a far different story. As a youngster he was once reprimanded for running around his mother's office during a company Christmas party, by a Rosanne Barr-lookalike who happened to be his mother's co-worker. His mother's kind and gentle boss did intervene and try to make him feel better via a hug and an open invite to come back and play whenever he liked and not to listen to the witch, but it was too late. He decided right then and there that real estate offices were not fun places and that stuck with him for over two decades.

Before he could get to the first desk, he heard Aubrey.

"What the fuck are you doing here?" she hissed, and made a beeline towards him.

"Look, I can explain," Michael began before he was expectedly cut off.

"Explain what? That making a few extra bucks at the expense of people you came to know and love was worth it? That you're no different than any other Tri-State type that uses the Cape for the summer, then doesn't give a fuck about it when it's no longer your seasonal playground?"

Aubrey began, as every realtor in the office now had their eyes fixed on the dueling duo. An open fight in the middle of a crowded office is something that doesn't happen too often, so this had all the appeal of a Hollywood blockbuster to Aubrey's co-workers.

"I bought the bar back. It's mine and Brendan's. Everything is going back to the way it was before the sale," Michael said, thinking that would calm her down.

Aubrey still wasn't buying what she assumed was his BS.

"Oh, so a guy from Wall Street spent a shit-load of money to impress a chick. So creative. What are you gonna tell me next? That you're swooping me off to New York City to live happily ever after on the banks of the Hudson?"

Now he knew he had her right where he wanted her.

"Well," he began, "that'll be pretty difficult, seeing as how I don't work on Wall Street anymore, nor do I even live in New York these days."

Her rage turned to disbelief in an instant as she crossed her arms and stared into Michael's soul. "Wait, so you're saying you threw it all away to own a bar in Wellfleet?"

"I wouldn't say I threw it away-I just elected to go in another direction," he said, as he tried to justify his move. "I just thought long and hard about what I had done and who it affected, and I wanted different things in life. The sale of The Whaler, coupled with the reality of life on Wall Street, became too much."

Aubrey's face dropped as her expression turned from rage to a sort of elated shock as she looked at Michael.

"Well, don't I feel like a bitch," Aubrey said as she realized her radio silence and little outburst weren't exactly justified. "Can I get my Friday nights and Saturday day shifts back?"

"I thought you'd never ask. I think the owner can definitely make that happen," Michael said as he made his first personnel move as the head honcho.

"My old apartment in Wellfleet got moved into last week. You know of anywhere I can crash down there?"

"I know a guy that's got a decent pad. Right above The Whaler, too."

"Sweet, tell him we'll figure out the sleeping arrangements later," Aubrey said, as she started packing up her still barely set-up desk. When her boss walked up to see what the situation was all Aubrey could do was laugh and say, "Joy, I quit."

Suffice is to say, her boss was more than slightly taken aback.

"I've been known as a hard-ass before, but this has to be a new record. In and out and less than a week. Wow. I thought you had some potential, too."

"I do have potential, just not the kind that makes it worth coming to work every day to sell condos to yuppies. Good fucking luck," Aubrey said, as the two made their way towards the door, like a much less violent Bonnie and Clyde.

After they left the realtor's office, they hopped into Michael's "new" ride. Aubrey was slightly impressed, not only that he now owned a truck, but it wasn't some gaudy "look at me" automobile.

"A Ford pickup? Holy hell, you really have changed," she said as he put the truck in drive.

"Where to?" Michael asked.

"This is all fucking crazy, but my apartment. Let's load this thing up and go *home*."

After loading up Aubrey's belongings (minus her bed, bureau and anything that was too heavy for the duo to carry), it was on the I-93 South, then Route 3 right to Cape Cod. Aubrey figured that the heavy stuff could stay behind, since she had paid rent for the next two months, so they could always come back later, or hire movers. "So much for renting condos to every yuppy asshole looking to break into the Southie social scene on their parents' dimes," Aubrey declared as she rolled down the window to take in some of the Indian Summer.

As Aubrey looked out the window into the traffic on Route 3 South to the Cape, she thought about her whirlwind past few months. "What are you thinking?" Michael asked as they were stuck in gridlock on the infamous Southeast Expressway.

"What a shitshow the last few months have been," Aubrey said.

"You're telling me."

"No. Seriously I spent I don't how much time planning on leaving the restaurant industry to make my parents proud, then I finally do it lasts a few weeks and I'm back. Plus I fell in love and that thing throws a wrinkle in damn near everything," Aubrey said as she crammed a few big time life events into a pair of sentences.

"Wait. You're in *love*? What's this guy's name?" Michael said as the traffic just began to break.

"It's not Michael O'Reilly," Aubrey said as she leaned in and kissed Michael, almost causing a major accident.

"Be careful," Michael said as maintained control of the car, "we've taken enough risks, can't have one too many.

The playfulness continued all the way to Cape Cod as they pulled into the lot of The Whaler like a pair of conquering heroes. A king and queen who had returned to rule their throne of vodka sodas and draft beers.

23

October 10-11

Given that the bar never officially closed having a "re-opening party" would sound kind of stupid, but it was under new management and it was staying open, and that was reason enough to celebrate. Michael tended his bar and was as happy opening a bottled beer as he was mixing one of the cocktails he had come up with. There were less than a dozen people in the place on this quiet Tuesday night when Michael decided to give back as only a bar owner can.

"Drinks are on me tonight or, shall I say, drinks are on the house tonight!"

"You need your co-owner to sign off on that before you do such crazy shit, Mike!" Brendan yelled from across the bar.

"Shit. I'm sorry-what's the verdict, lieutenant?" Michael asked sarcastically as he moved towards Brendan's barstool.

"Give the people what they want!" Brendan said as he too got to get a rise out of the small, but passionate crowd in the bar this fall evening.

"By the way, boss, it's not in the paperwork, but our deal about Charlie Coyle having his Stanley Cup party here is still on the table, right? We all know the miserable fucking bastard that used to own this place would just as soon die before letting a hockey function go on in here."

"Sure. But the only way that kid is winning a damn Stanley Cup this season is if he's traded to the Rangers."

"Well, if that's the case he'd need a time machine back to 1994 for that to happen," Brendan replied, putting some salt in the wound of the New Yorker.

"Such a dick, dude."

Michael replied as he moved on from Brendan to where Aubrey was behind the bar. Hockey talk was cool and all, but not even dreams of Stanley Cup glory could come close to her.

Aubrey was pouring a draft beer as Michael made his way towards her and the always bubbly bartender was even more bubbly once her boss/lover sat himself right beside her.

"What's up, stud?" she asked as she gave the beer to a waiting customer before doubling back to where Michael was.

"In that whole journey down here this afternoon I never asked you, what caused *your* change of heart?" Michael calmly and directly asked her.

"Which one?" she asked, since she'd had a few changes of heart with Michael since he walked into this bar and her life on that April night.

"The one where you went from swearing off dating coworkers and bosses to kissing me on the beach and quitting making your parents happy to go back to slinging beers."

"Oh. *That* one," Aubrey said. "I saw you go from being a machine programmed to only think about the bottom line to being someone who cared for the people around him. Of course, you reverted to your old ways for a hot second. But at the end of the day, you more than redeemed yourself."

"I guess a leopard can change his spots, after all."

"I thought it was a tiger's stripes?" Aubrey replied as she wasn't sure if he was getting his big cat idioms confused.

"Leopard. Tiger. What's the difference? Although I will say only one of them knows how to hold a golf club."

"Always have to get a joke in there, don't ya?"

"You'll get used to it. I promise," Michael answered with his almost devilish grin.

"You better hope to god I do, or else," Aubrey replied as she shot him a smile and moved on to help a pair of guests a few seats down.

The place never got busy that night and that was fine as they didn't need a big crowd to celebrate a new day in town. When it was time to close up Michael, Brendan, Aubrey, and Christina sat at the bar with the doors locked long into the night, exchanging stories and having laughs as a new era was unofficially ushered in. There would be no more geriatric owner barking out orders that were often counterproductive, nor would there be a sale hanging over the place. There was now young, intelligent management and ownership and a great deal of stability in The Whaler that gave it a feeling of warmth that it had lacked for a long time. When they did leave for the night, it was almost 3 am, and while Christina and Brendan headed for the door, Michael and Aubrey made their way upstairs to what was now *their* apartment.

The sun began creeping through the window and hit Aubrey's back at an angle that could blind you if you looked at it directly. Michael got up and headed towards the bedroom window which gave him a perfect view of Cape Cod Bay. Under different circumstances, he'd have been a world away getting ready to traverse the urban jungle to close deals on Wall Street. That world, though far away, was still on his mind as he settled into his new life on the coast of Massachusetts. Looking out one last time before he went to get set for another day, he chuckled, took one look at the love of his life, and said to himself, "It's gonna be a great fucking day."

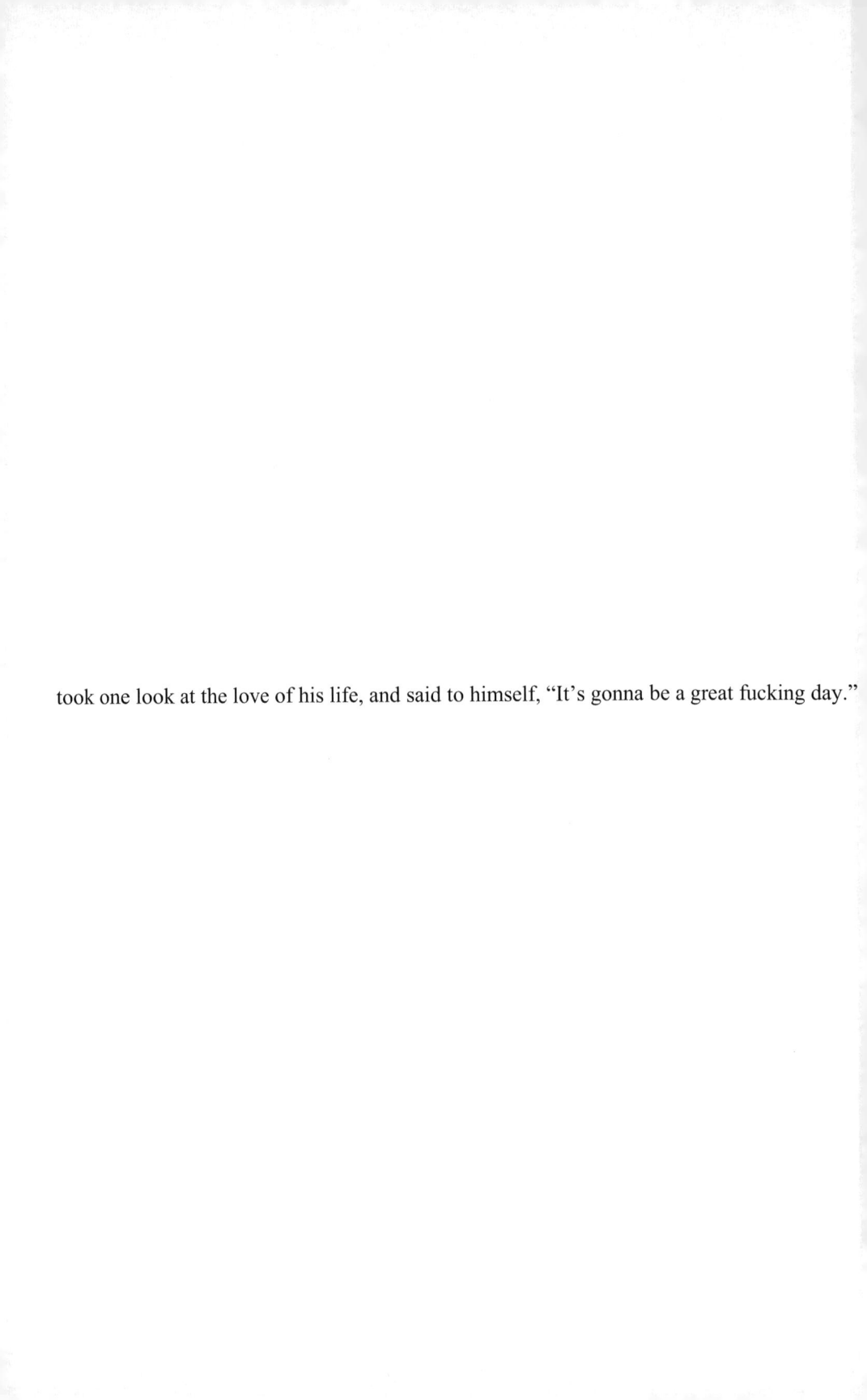

Made in the USA
Middletown, DE
28 June 2017